INEVITABLE DECEPTIONS

The Heart's Journey to Nowhere 2

By

Sheena Perry

D1444525

SHEENA PERRY

Copyright

Inevitable Deceptions 2

Copyright © 2018 Sheena Perry

Published by Sheena Perry

Edited by Sheena Perry

ISBN: 0-9986999-2-6
ISBN-13: 978-0-9986999-2-9

INEVITABLE DECEPTIONS 2

The *Tea* on the Author

Sheena Perry is originally from Dallas, TX. She was raised by her teenage single mother, Tonya. Sheena is the oldest of two children. Sheena's mother fell prey to the booming crack cocaine era of the 1980's. Entrusting a close relative with the task of babysitting her two kids, Tonya left for work one day not realizing that the family member would leave them alone and call DCFS.

At tender age of three, Sheena and her brother were removed from the home and placed into separate foster homes. While her brother was placed into a fairly nice foster home, she however suffered unimaginable abuse at the hands of her foster parents. She went days without eating, was fed dog food and she was tied to a chair throughout the day. Her thighs are still branded with the markings from the tight ropes.

Her mother was able to quickly regain custody of both children. However, later the same year she was molested by her mother's fiancé. Immediately reporting the abuse to her mother, the monster was quickly apprehended and served a lengthy stint in prison. Prison did not stop Sheena's molester from issuing out death threats.

He was heavily involved in the drug world and his threats were taken very seriously. Sheena's mom relocated her small family to Columbus, GA. After experiencing such traumatic events, she became extremely shy and withdrawn. She was even mute for two years. The once bubbly outgoing little girl had been replaced by an insecure, self-loathing shell of her former self.

As she became older, Sheena would contemplate suicide numerous times to cope with the unfortunate cards she had been dealt. She had even developed an eating disorder in her mid-teens. Sheena's mother continued to battle with her drug addiction throughout her childhood and into her young adulthood. Sheena has always had a deep passion for reading and writing. Reading has always been her outlet to escape the obstacles that she faced on a daily basis.

She enjoys romance, mystery, horror, autobiographies, thrillers and urban novels. From an early age, Sheena had tutored kids much older than herself. Sheena particularly enjoys writing short stories and poetry. She currently lives in Florissant, MO. Despite her rough beginnings, she was able to conquer all of her hurdles and meet many of her goals.

She was able to purchase her first house at the age of 20. A year later she gave birth to her daughter, Aaliyah. Somehow, she managed to overcome the murder of her daughter's father, who was killed by the police when their daughter was just 4 months old. She is a Registered Nurse. Sheena has a Master's degree in Nursing Education. She is currently in school pursing her Doctorate degree.

She works as a nursing professor at a major university and is the Director of Nursing at a long-term care facility. Sheena is also a licensed foster parent. Having had such a horrific experience during her time in foster care, she wanted to offer a safe home to children in need. Please tuned for **Inevitable Deceptions: The Heart's Journey to Nowhere 3** which is Sheena's third and final installment of this series. She also cowrote the children's book **I Made You From Scratch: You Are Perfect** with her daughter. She is currently working on **My Wife's Daughters**. She has also published novels such as **The Girl Behind The Smile** by Dornisha Goodrich and **God Showed Me More Than Heaven** by K.S. Fisher. Please stay tuned!

I attribute my success to this – I never gave or took any excuse. – Florence Nightingale

Connect with Sheena

Visit her website at www.sheenaperrypublishing.com

Friend her on Facebook at www.facebook.com/sheena.p.rn

Link with her on LinkedIn at
www.linkedin.com/in/sheena-perry-msn-rn-cne-22352486

Follow her on Twitter at www.twitter.com/sheenamperry

Follow her on Instagram at www.instagram.com/sheenamperry

You can also visit her business page at
https://m.facebook.com/SheenaPerryPublishing/

Submissions for all genres are now open. Please submit the first 3-4 chapters of your manuscript for publishing consideration. Allow up to 30 days for a response. Complete contact information including name, address, contact number and email. Use 12 pt. font, double-spaced in manuscript style format. Email manuscripts to submissions@sheenaperrypublishing.com.

Or mail manuscript to:

Sheena Perry Publishing
P.O. Box 947
Florissant, MO 63032

We look forward to hearing from you!

Dedication

I'd like to dedicate this book to all of those who have been on the receiving end of abuse. Always know that it is never your fault. You are not alone. Don't be ashamed. Be your own advocate; seek help immediately before it is too late. Do not let your abuser have power over you. Remember that if they've abused you once, chances are that they will strike again.

In loving memory of Michael Calvin Perry, Doris Marie Green, Carolyn Marie White, James Green, Samuel Keita DeBoise, Erin LeighAnna Nabe, Lennette Berry and Michael Perry Jr.

I love and miss you all more than anyone will ever know. Rest in paradise.

~Sheena

Table of Contents

Acknowledgements

To my loving mother, Tonya Perry, I appreciate you for always being my biggest cheerleader. You have always inspired me to challenge myself. You are the strongest person that I know. I love you so much Ma!

To my brother, Rico, we may not always see eye to eye but know that I will always love you to the moon and back. No one can make me laugh the way that you do. You are my best friend.

To my beautiful daughter, Aaliyah, the day that I had you was by far the happiest day of my life. You made me grow up overnight. You are growing into the most amazing young woman that I could ever ask for. I know that your dad is smiling down at you from heaven. I hope that I have always been a positive role model for you and that you realize that you are my biggest motivator. All of my accomplishments were achieved with you in mind. Remember the sky is the limit and that the word *never* is not a part of our vocabulary. I love you baby girl.

To my friends and colleagues that have put up with my endless brainstorms and offered words of encouragement, I thank you for everything. I'd also like to thank my test readers who have given me constructive criticism.

I'd also like to give a special thanks to my readers who have purchased, downloaded and rated my books. You will never know how much your love and support means to me.

Lastly, I'd like to thank the good Lord above. Thank you for continuing to bless me. Without you, none of this would be possible.

~Sheena

INEVITABLE DECEPTIONS 2

« Prologue »

The Past "Alicia"

NOW THAT I WAS NO longer devastated over our breakup, I had resumed my workouts. I was walking around a nearby track, trying to remain as active as I could. Two miles into my walk, I decided to take a quick break.

I was out of breath and greedily gulping my water. Suddenly someone roughly bumped into me making me spill water down my chin and onto my shirt. I was immediately pissed off. How could anyone not see my big pregnant ass standing here drinking my water?! To make matters worse, they didn't even have the home training to say 'excuse me'.

As I turned around to see who the ass wipe was, I was quickly pushed onto the ground. Lying on my back, I finally got a good look at who was fucking with me. Tamar and a short brown skin girl were standing over me and screaming obscenities.

Tamar furiously pushed me back onto the ground each time I attempted to stand up. She then began to rain blows all over my face and body. My protruding belly was not spared from the vicious attack. I defended myself the best that I could. Had I not been pregnant, she wouldn't have been a match for me.

At eight months pregnant, I was in no condition to fight. My primary concern was protecting my round midsection. The other girl just stood there watching Tamar's attack against me. While she didn't participate in the attack, she did nothing to stop it either. She looked almost remorseful, yet she did nothing to help me or my son. For that, I owed her a generous ass whooping once I delivered my son.

As Tamar continued to rain blows all over my body, I prayed for God to intervene in some way. She was now pulling chunks of my hair out from my scalp. I was in total agony.

After she grew tired she hocked up a massive loogie and decorated my battered face with it. Then her crazy ass produced a razor from nowhere and proceeded to carve a long slit into my right cheek. I knew that cut would never disappear. She then started unevenly chopping my hair off with the blade. When I looked at her, I only saw pure evil.

She then stated, "Bitch you just couldn't stay away from Mike, could you?! He is my man and I don't give a shit about that bastard inside of you. I bet your skank ass is the one who burned him, causing him to burn me. You nasty hoe! You're the reason why he doesn't want to be with me and our daughter. You're a distraction. You are a scandalous, homewrecking little bitch!

Unfortunately for you, you must be eliminated. I'm sick of competing with your high-sadity ass. It's a wrap for you hoe. I doubt that he'll want you now that I've fucked up your face...but I have to make sure. I refuse to allow you to have my man's son. I'm sorry, but I just can't. Perhaps in another lifetime, you and I could've been friends."

She then snatched the other girl's purse off her shoulder.

"Alicia, lucky for you I'm not into torturing people. Your death will be quick and painless. And so will his," she stated pointing the gun at my abdomen.

Through my swollen lips, I begged, "Look Tamar, I haven't talked to Mike in over four months. After I found out about you, I left him for good. I don't want anything to do with him anymore. Please just let us go. I'll stay away from him forever. No one has to get hurt. It isn't worth it. Between me and you, this isn't even his baby." I lied, desperate for her to end her relentless attack.

"Bitch, do I look stupid to you?! Hey Shay, do you hear this broad over here?" She scoffed to her friend.

She continued, "I know you are still fucking with Mike. He rarely comes home anymore. He hasn't been by to see me or his daughter in two weeks because he has been laying up under your fat ass!" With that she callously kicked me in my stomach.

I doubled over in excruciating pain. I felt terrible for my son. I hadn't felt him move in a while and he was typically very active. Following the kick, I felt a gush of fluid trickling out of my vagina. It was a mixture of amniotic fluid and blood. Fuck! I can't be going into labor now!

"Please! I'm not lying. You need to get me to a hospital! My water just broke. I promise that I haven't seen Mike in months. Please don't do this!" I begged.

Ignoring me she replied, "I'm sorry, but it's already done. Rest in hell, bitch!!!" She screamed as I felt hot lead pierce through my stomach, followed by another bullet being lodged into my chest.

TO BE CONTINUED...

« Chapter 1 Sincere »

The Past "Alicia"

DEATH DEFINITELY PUT a lot of things into prospective. I had never been a religious person, but I considered myself to be somewhat spiritual. My best friend Cee Cee always tried talking me into going to church with her, but I just could not see myself waking up early every week day and then waking up early on the weekend too! That simply was not happening!

In the past, I'd often wonder about the afterlife, reincarnations and what heaven would be like. After being shot twice by Tamar, I knew that my time here on Earth had ended. I had never felt pain like that before. It all appeared to be happening in slow motion. I remember excruciating pain, followed by numbness and then a feeling of drowsiness.

After that, my memories became fragmented. I recall drifting in and out of consciousness. After she filled me with hot lead and left me to die, Tamar and her friend, Shay, cowardly ran off.

My next memory is of EMS workers performing CPR on me. I was peering down from above and watching the scene unfold. My battered face was unrecognizable. My warm blood stained the hot pavement below me. I had lost so much blood. As I looked on, I could see the worried expressions on their faces.

As the third EMT took over compressions, I quickly heard him yell out, "Fuck, I just cracked one of her ribs!"

However, he didn't allow that little mishap to slow down his rate of compressions. I continued to look on as another worker proceeded to insert an IV into my right hand. Their resuscitative efforts lasted for what seemed like an eternity. I knew that in most cases they would have stopped by now. However, who wanted to call it quits when there was a pregnant woman involved? No one wanted to carry that baggage around with them.

I felt that I was losing grip on my physical self. The distance between the scene and my current existence was growing. I was moving rapidly through this place. Becoming dizzy, I snapped my weary eyes shut. After what felt like hours, I felt a light tap on my right shoulder. Quickly opening my eyes, I gasped at the most beautiful scenery that I'd ever laid my eyes on.

After marveling at my blissful surroundings, I focused in on the person who'd tapped me on the shoulder. My eyes grew as big as saucers once I saw a few familiar faces before me. My late step-father, Tony, was proudly beaming at me. Behind him stood my grandparents and my little cousin Sweetie who had passed away in a drowning accident.

Surprisingly, I was not fearful. I actually felt at peace. I felt as if I belonged here. There was no more pain, fear, embarrassment, jealousy or hatred. I was consumed with joy and contentment. I was surrounded by love and reunited with those with only good intentions.

"Am I...dead?" I whispered.

"Alicia baby, what are you doing here? It isn't your time. You have to go back!" Tony replied.

He continued, "Don't get me wrong baby girl, we have all missed you tremendously, but you simply cannot stay here."

I looked him over. He was wearing his military attire and looked handsome as ever.

"But I don't want to go back there. There is too much evil there. I have never felt better. Can I please stay here with you?!" I cried.

My grandmother motioned for me to come over to her.

"Sweet Pea, you are still needed on Earth. Your journey isn't over. My great-grandson needs you and so does my daughter. If you don't return, it will kill your mother. She has already lost a husband. Please go back and FIGHT!" She coaxed.

I burst into tears. "I miss all of you. I don't want to leave you. Please don't make me leave. Come back with me." I sniffled.

My grandfather had always been a man of few words; however, he finally spoke up, "Alicia, you know if we could come back with you, we would. Our missions were all completed on Earth. The good Lord needs our services here. When it is your time, we will see you again. But you've got to go now before it's too late!"

Before I was able to respond, I recall getting closer to my physical self again. Looking down, I watched as my son was cut from my abdomen. He was quickly whisked away to what I presumed was the NICU.

He was so tiny, so innocent, so beautiful. I knew then that my family was right. I couldn't leave him behind. I just prayed that he made it. He wasn't breathing properly when they extracted him from my womb. My last recollections were of me fervently praying for God to save my little Prince.

∞

As I slowly opened my eyes, a feeling of foreboding consumed me. I did not recognize my surroundings and instantly began to panic. I attempted to sit up until I was paralyzed by agonizing pain. I felt as if I had been run over by a truck. It was difficult for me to see out of my right eye. I could also feel a bandage on the right side of my face. My head was pounding something fierce. As I surveyed the room, I saw my mother and Cee Cee sitting next to my bed with worried expressions etched on their pretty faces.

Cee Cee noticed that I was awake first and ran to my side. I cleared my dry throat and managed to ask, "Baby?"

"Alicia, do you remember what happened?" My mother asked.

I cautiously shook my head in pain. I remembered, however, I didn't want to let on that I knew who my attacker was.

"A good Samaritan noticed your battered body lying on Grant's Trail and called for assistance. You were unresponsive when help arrived. You were beaten, your face was cut, your hair was chopped off and you were shot. Between the attack and CPR, you have sustained multiple fractured ribs. You were shot twice, once in your abdomen and once in your chest.

Luckily both bullets missed your vital organs and the baby. They went straight through. The most damage was caused by your head being kicked and banged onto the ground. It resulted in a lot of swelling to your brain. You went into premature labor shortly after being attacked at the park. They had to perform an emergency cesarean section on you..."

"Baby???!!!" I squealed through clenched teeth.

After hesitating my mom stated, "The baby is in the NICU. He was having some difficulty with his breathing. It was touch and go for a while, but the doctors are hopeful that everything will be fine. They had to give him steroids and surfactant therapy to help his lungs mature faster. You've done such a great job Alicia, he is perfect!

It is you that had us worried to death. You've been in a medically induced coma for the past nine days due to the swelling in your brain. We were told that whoever attacked you had banged your head on the ground multiple times. Who would do something like this Alicia? Were you robbed?"

I shook my head and whispered, "I can't really remember mom. It's all extremely vague. I just remember taking a break from walking and then everything just went black. If they came to rob me, jokes on them. I only had ten dollars on me."

"I wonder if Mike had something to do with this," Cee Cee stated.

"No Cee Cee, I don't think that even Mike is this evil. Besides, he wanted the baby. He wouldn't have risked harming him." I replied.

My mom reasoned, "Alicia you need to report any details that you can recall to the police. No matter how small. They've been coming every day to see if you had been brought out of your coma. Everyone was afraid that you wouldn't remember the incident due to the severity of your head injuries.

Don't worry baby, the doctors assured us that eventually your short-term memories will return. It's a miracle! I have half a mind to kill this animal myself! They are lucky that I have a nursing license to maintain. Otherwise I'd personally kick his or her ass for this. Everyone knows not to fuck with me or mine!"

"Ma, please don't get worked up over this. I don't even want to think about whoever did this right now. All I want is some breath mints and I want to go visit my son. Can you two take me to see him? I hope he looks like me and not that slut bucket of a father of his," I joked attempting to lighten the mood.

"We can do that, but first we need to let the doctor know that you're finally awake," my mother stated seriously.

∞

After receiving a thorough head to toe assessment, the hospital staff were convinced that I wasn't suffering from any long-term neurological damage. I received pain medication and was given an ice pack to help reduce the edema that had claimed my face. Being a respected nurse at the hospital, my mom had pulled some strings.

She was able to get me the best plastic surgeon to work on my face while I was still in a coma. She was assured that the cut would be practically gone within a year. I was hopeful. My ribs were wrapped tightly which limited my movements substantially. My cesarean incision wasn't as painful as I knew it probably had been nine days ago.

My mom and Cee Cee refused to allow me to see my face. They were fearful of my reaction. I trusted their judgement and was well aware that I had to look like fly covered shit. Actually, that is exactly how I felt as well. I swear those bitches would pay for what they had done to me. I had never wronged either of them. There was a special place in hell reserved for the both of them. I was just thankful that I had been blessed with a relatively healthy baby.

It pained me that I was not awake for his birth. My mom and Cee Cee were not permitted to be present for the birth either, given the circumstances. I had security outside of my room twenty-four hours a day. Because of my severe injuries, they feared my attacker would come back to finish me off upon discovering that I was still alive. Deep down I knew their assumptions were correct. Tamar was definitely going to be coming back for me...only this time I'd be prepared for that ass!

I had a detailed birth plan prepared and was unable to fulfill any of my requests...thankfully my mom did have my baby boy circumcised for me. That was an absolute must. No son of mine would ever be caught wearing a turtleneck!

As my mom wheeled me down to the neonatal intensive care unit, I felt my heart begin to race. I don't know why but my little baby had me so intimidated. I wondered if he would instantly bond with me. Had I missed that window of opportunity? Would he recognize my voice, my touch or scent? I had planned to breastfeed him, was that still an option?

Once we made it onto the unit, I nervously grabbed and squeezed Cee Cee's hand. I wasn't sure what to expect. I prayed that he wasn't hooked up to all the tubes that some of the other babies were. In a room full of seemingly identical babies, I instantly knew my son when I laid eyes on him. He was the most precious baby that I had ever been privileged enough to see.

I'm not just saying that because he was mine either! He was gorgeous! My heart melted and the water works began to flood my battered face. He was perfect, just as my mom had claimed. Despite the pain, I stood from the wheelchair and limped over to my son. Wow, did I just say *my son*. I went through the motions of counting his fingers and toes. I removed his baby hat, onesie and his diaper.

I wanted to memorize every inch of my baby. He was a beautiful mixture of both Mike and I. He had my eyes, dimples, hair and complexion. He had Mike's nose, ears, cleft chin and his lips. He even had the same cherry shaped birthmark on his shoulder blade as Mike. It amazed me how two very different people could combine their DNA and recreate altered, yet improved extensions of themselves.

I found out that he weighed four pounds and fourteen ounces and was seventeen inches long at birth. My mom told me that while I was in the coma, she had called Mike and he had been coming up daily to visit our baby. However, she did not permit him to visit me. I was grateful for that.

She stated that Mike had been pushing her to name our son after him. She had told him that no decisions regarding his name would be made until after I woke up. Staring into my son's eyes that looked just like mine, the perfect name came to mind.

"His name is going to be Sincere. Sincere Michael Anderson."

"I like that," they both replied in unison.

I decided to take the high road. Although I was laid up in a hospital bed behind Mike and he had hurt me in ways beyond my comprehension, I still considered his feelings. While I did not make our son a junior, I had still incorporated his name and gave Sincere his last name. As the three of us sat back admiring my son, I knew that I had made the right decision. Was my "out of body experience" real or a figment of my imagination? I didn't know how to bring it up to my mom and Cee Cee without sounding like a lunatic.

In the mere moments that I'd been with my son, I felt my heart swell. I now knew what unconditional love was. There was nothing that my little guy could ever do to diminish my love for him. We instantly connected and I knew that he was aware that I was his mother. I instinctively placed my baby boy to my breast and he immediately latched on. The world was tuned out as I sang to my sweet boy until he fell asleep in my arms.

« Chapter 2 H2O »

The Past "Gladys"

WALKING AWAY FROM Lukas was one of the most difficult decisions that I had ever had to make. I considered myself to be a fairly open-minded person, however, Lukas just had too many difficult pills to swallow. Although I went about business as usual, I thought about him continuously. He invaded my mind so often that I was convinced that he had hexed me.

I couldn't categorize what we had as a breakup, because we were never *technically* together. If love and heartbreak felt anything like this, then I wanted no parts of that mess. I think the most difficult part of it all was the fact that I had become so use to having him around, to never seeing him at all. He never hung around the neighborhood anymore either.

As much as I missed him, I had to stick to my guns and move on. Eventually, I made the decision to move on campus. I'd concluded that I would only experience the college life once and I wanted to live it to the fullest. I was no fool, I kept my family home as well, hell it was paid off! I'd stop by the house every Sunday after church just to check mail and to ensure that things were in order. It was in my new dorm room that I met Shawn's mother, Paige.

We quickly became close friends. She was majoring in accounting. She was one of the most intelligent people that I had ever met. On another note, she could also be a bit of a wild child. She was a green-eyed, smoking hot brunette beauty. She was extremely petite with large breasts. She had lips so full that she would've given Angelina Jolie a run for her money. She was five foot one and weighed about one hundred and fifteen pounds. Despite her small frame, guys were drawn to her magnetic beauty. They were literally lined around the corner trying to hook up with her.

Unfortunately, none of them had to put in much work. There was a different guy in and out of our room almost every night. She never really seemed to care about the fact that I was a mere few feet away from her freaky sex sessions. She'd still bellow out soprano worthy moans while I tried to feign sleep. Somehow, I had learned to tune out the animalistic grunts of pleasure. None of the guys ever really lasted too long, so I was okay with that.

Once I got to know her better, she had told me that she paid her tuition with the money that she collected from her many sex partners. In some strange way, that made me feel a little better. At least she was having sex for a positive purpose. I just thought the heifer was a nympho! Aside from our dorm room being a virtual brothel, Paige was cool to have as a roommate.

She always paid her portion of the bills on time and was very clean. What more could I ask for? My acceptance of her undercover profession made me feel like a hypocrite in a way. I'd walked away from Luke for exploiting women who had the same occupation.

In Lukas's absence, I had been hanging out with Omar more. He was a great guy. Whenever I was in his presence, he'd have me laughing until my cheeks hurt. I always cherished our time together. He was pre-med and had an extremely busy schedule.

Although he came from a successful family, he was determined to get through school independently. He struggled to make ends meet like most of the students on campus. He worked at a local casino and he also worked part-time at the school we attended. He inspired me in so many ways.

During one of our dates, he asked me how I felt about meeting his family. Naturally, I was shocked and giddy with excitement. No guy had ever introduced me to their family before. I guess he was serious about me. I was so flattered as I wallowed on cloud nine internally.

"When can I meet your family Omar?" I asked.

"We are heading over there now. I've told them all about the beautiful Gladys who swept their son off his feet. They've been wanting to meet you for some time now. I just wasn't sure if you were ready." He concluded.

"I would be honored to meet your family baby. How do I look?" I asked.

"You're almost as pretty as me girl!" He joked as I lightly punched his chiseled arm.

∞

Omar's parents were amazing. Despite being very important people, they welcomed me with open arms and made me feel like a part of their family. They lived out in Wentzville and I was impressed by their lovely home. His parents were down to Earth and never made me feel less than. After leaving his parent's house, Omar suggested that we hang out at my house. He claimed that we never had any privacy in either of our dorm rooms.

He could only afford to rent a place that housed several guys to a room. There definitely wasn't any privacy at his place. I shrugged and agreed to go with the flow. I was still so happy to have met his parents. Before reaching my house, Omar stopped by one of the many liquor stores in the neighborhood. He knew that I loved Bailey's, so that's what he purchased for the evening.

Once reaching my house, I made us some popcorn, while he made our drinks. We both opted to watch comedies. We sipped, laughed and munched on the popcorn. Soon I was feeling great. Apparently, he was too. As we sat blanketed and cuddled up on my sofa, I felt his hand creep onto my unclad thigh. He then proceeded to softly caress it. My clit instantly started throbbing. My breathing quickened and my nipples hardened. I prayed that he hadn't noticed.

I was feeling electricity flowing throughout my entire body.

"Gladys, turn around. I want to give you a back massage." Omar ordered.

I was feeling great and saw no harm in an innocent back massage. His hands were so relaxing. He relieved the tension that I had in my neck, back and rear end. He massaged me so thoroughly and for so long that I felt myself drifting off to sleep.

Soon I felt Omar rolling me onto my back. He leaned forward and he gave me some warm, passionate kisses. I found myself seductively biting on his bottom lip and sucking on his tongue like a miniature penis. I then clumsily pulled him on top of me. I had no idea what I was doing, but it felt so right in that moment. I wanted Omar to make love to me on that couch.

I was wearing a nightgown and some black lace panties. As Omar gyrated his hips into mine, I could feel his erection poking teasingly at my center. I whimpered uncontrollably every time his pipe would stab my clit. It was driving me crazy. I never wanted those sensations to end. Through it all, we continued to kiss aggressively.

Standing up to remove his pants, Omar said, "Damn G, you soaked my pants. Look at this big ass wet spot." He smirked.

Embarrassed, I through a pillow at him. Then I covered my head with my cover.

"Girl, what are you hiding for?! That's the sexiest shit I've ever seen. I like that. It means your body likes me." He bragged while removing the cover from my head.

I remained silent. He continued to remove his pants as I looked on. He had an amazing body. His magic stick was a little larger than average. Plenty for me, but I'm sure a big 'coochied' woman might not have been completely satisfied with Omar's length and girth.

Due to the alcohol, I didn't have the energy to move. Omar came over to me and removed my sopping wet panties. Climbing between my limp legs, Omar asked me to put his dick inside of me. Not thinking about contraceptives, I did as I was told. I placed his intermediate sized wood at the entrance of my opening.

Omar proceeded to slowly work his length into my tight wet box. It was very uncomfortable, but not excruciating as other women claimed it would be. Then again, maybe the alcohol was alleviating some of the discomfort. I gripped onto Omar's back as he continued to open me up. His moans were those of a man in paradise. His pace sped up as he slid his hands underneath my ass, allowing him to drill deeper into me.

I glanced up at his face to find his eyes closed. His handsome face was distorted into an ugly expression. He definitely needed to adopt more attractive sex faces, I thought as I held back my giggles. It had started to feel extremely good. I had begun to thrust upwards in order to match his strokes. I was on the verge of cumming when I noticed that his pace had drastically quickened.

I was paralyzed by the rapid pace. The next thing I knew, his body became stiff. He made sporadic jerking movements as he howled at the top of his lungs. I wasn't sure how to feel about any of it. Frankly, I was a little turned off. I was still horny but he'd made my rising orgasm disappear with the ugly faces and comical acoustics.

I felt his dick become soft inside of me. He was sweaty and breathing heavily as he slowly pulled his member out of me. As I glanced at the VCR, I realized that we had been only been going at it for a whopping four minutes!

Sexually frustrated, drunk, tired and dripping semen, I darted into the bathroom. I turned the water on to a warm setting. Once I was satisfied with the temperature, I climbed in.

Sitting in the tub, I laid down onto my back. I then scooted my plump ass down to the end of the tub. With my legs spread wide open, I ensured that the water was streaming down directly onto my clit. Immediately, I was in a state of ecstasy. As the H2O worked wonders on my pearl, I commenced to pinching my milk chocolate nipples. Before long, I started feeling my orgasm return.

Imagining Omar being inside of me just a few minutes ago, pushed me over the edge.

"Sssssssss! Fuck! Oh God! It feels so damn GOOD!!!" I hissed, shaking uncontrollably.

Finally satiated, I glanced down at my sore twat. "Now why couldn't he take care of you the way that water did? If that is sex, it is certainly overrated!" I mumbled breathlessly.

My pussy had been thirsty, yet he was unable to quench *her* thirst. Drying off, I thought of how the *thought* of Omar turned me on more than *he* actually did. It was time for him to go!

« Chapter 3 Baby Mama Woes »

The Past "Mike"

WHAT A SHITTY PAST year! My life has been unbelievable lately. I wasn't on good terms with either of my kid's mothers right now. I hated that shit too. Don't get me wrong, I was grateful that I was the father of a healthy baby boy and a beautiful baby girl. I was just stressed out. I was fresh out of high school, but now had two kids merely months apart. I felt like a million things were coming at me all at once, but I tried to take it all in stride. My family wasn't too happy with me, but they welcomed my babies with open arms.

I was still the man out there on the basketball court and on the football field. I never lost focus of the bottom line. Not surprisingly, I received a football scholarship at a nearby university. It was tough, but it was all for my kids. I couldn't afford to fail. Let me go back to the day that Alicia saw me with Tamar and my baby girl Michaela. I felt my entire world collapse around me.

I couldn't believe that I had gotten caught out in the open like that. The look of betrayal and devastation that was etched on Alicia's face that day still continues to haunt me. For the first time ever, I saw hate in her eyes for me. There was so much that I wanted to say to her, but I knew in that moment it would've only fallen on deaf ears.

Plus, I didn't want to cause a scene in front of my daughter. I knew I shouldn't have listened to Tamar's ass. I tried to be happy with Tamar, but honestly, she just wasn't good enough. I had started drinking more and reminded Tamar every chance I got that she was merely my second option.

She always wanted to go out and be seen with her attention seeking ass. It took everything in me not to chase after Alicia that day. I somehow managed to restrain myself and tried to act unaffected. After we left the mall, I dropped Michaela off over at my crib so that my mom could watch her. My mom ran a twenty-four hour home daycare so she always had a house full of kids.

Tamar and I then drove over to her place. As soon as her front door closed behind us, I walked up behind Tamar and wrapped my large hands around her thin neck. I squeezed tightly, even picking her up off the ground a little until she was on her tip-toes.

I couldn't see her face because her back was facing me. After a few moments, I slightly loosened my grip after noticing that she wasn't putting up much of a fight. I then body slammed her onto the hardwood floor. She looked up at me with absolute terror in her eyes.

Raising my right hand, preparing to cave the right side of her face in, I heard, "Mike, please! Don't hit me! I'm sorry for whatever it is that I've done to upset you. Baby, just talk to me, okay?" She pleaded.

"Bitch, I'm going to ask you this shit one time and one time only. Did you know that Alicia and Cee Cee were going to be at the mall today?" I barked.

"Hell no, Mike! How would I have known that they were going to be there? I don't talk to either of those bitches. Besides, why would I bring any drama around my fucking baby?!" She exclaimed rubbing her bruised neck.

"You mean *our* muthafucking baby and you better watch

your tone and how you speak to me bitch. I'm not one of those soft ass niggas that you're use to talking reckless to," I snapped.

"Okay, okay, I'm sorry. Take it easy. I'm just offended that you would think I planned that shit earlier. You know me better than that. You have me and La La now...why do you continue to chase behind Alicia anyway? I love you Mike. Why am I always put on the back burner?"

"Tamar, you know that I have love for you and that I love the fuck out of La La. What you need to understand is that Alicia is my future wife. I am *in* love with her. You knew what time it was when you and I started messing around again. I hope you didn't think that having La La was going to make me feel any differently about you because I don't. As you know, my girl is pregnant right now and can't handle any unnecessary stress. You know I'll always have your back and make sure that you and our daughter is straight," I stated truthfully.

She stared at me with pained eyes before responding, "I'm happy you finally put it out in the open. Now I know exactly where we stand. It's time for me to move on and find a guy who loves me as much as you love Alicia. I'm done loving and chasing someone who is in love with someone else. I'm done competing Mike. It's getting late. Can you take me back to your house so that I can pick up La La?"

I'll be honest, I wanted to knock Tamar on her ass for mentioning moving on with another nigga, but I knew that was just the selfish part of me. The logical part of me knew I had no right to be upset with her for wanting to date other people, but I was. She was still *my* bitch, even if she didn't occupy my number one spot!

"Tamar, you're talking dumb now. You know if you are fucking around with other people that I can't get down with you like that, right? And don't you ever bring another man around my baby. I mean that shit! If you are fucking with other niggas then they can foot the bills around here as well. I'll take care of my daughter, but I'm not going to pay the bills here if you're fucking other people. Your new nigga should be able to handle that.

Think about that before you start throwing your little pussy around. La La is cool where she's at. Now come over here, apologize and please daddy," I said massaging the bulge in my basketball shorts.

Rolling her eyes, she stood up and walked to her front door.

She opened the door and stated, "I meant what I said Mike. I'm not entertaining this anymore. You've made it perfectly clear who you want to be with...so be with her. I'll have my cousin take me to pick up Michaela in the morning."

With a bruised ego, I silently walked past Tamar. I roughly bumped her with my shoulder before mumbling, "Fucking bitch."

I saw red when I heard her ass reply, "Your fat ass momma." She then slammed and locked the door. Of course, I had a key to get in and bust her ass, but I had bigger fish to fry at the moment.

I didn't have time to play with her. I knew she was just in her feelings right now and would calm down eventually. She needed me. Truthfully, that is what I feared the most about Alicia. She didn't need me. I knew I needed to do something to get her to hear me out.

Just as I knew she would, Alicia was dodging my black ass like a bullet. It hurt like a muthafucka when she changed the ultrasound date and didn't allow me to find out what we were having. That shit was beyond foul!

Neither Cee Cee or Alicia's mom would let me near her. Those bitches monitored her more closely than the secret service. She had even stopped going to school. I waited outside of her classes for weeks, before I realized she wasn't going back. I was going crazy without her. I had pulled out all my tricks. I sent cards, flowers, candy and jewelry, but she wouldn't budge.

I came by every day, but she would never come to the door. I knew she was in there because sometimes the curtains would move. My baby was more of a homebody, where would she be going with my baby inside of her? I just knew one thing for sure; her stubborn ass better not make me miss the birth of our baby. I was hoping for a junior. I didn't think that I could handle another girl.

I had been fucking with Sha'Keisha for a while behind both Alicia and Tamar's backs. I had nearly pistol whooped that hoe to death. That nasty ass hoe had the nerve to burn me. There was no telling how long I had been walking around with that shit. I just prayed that I hadn't passed that shit on to either of them.

I had always strapped up with Sha'Keisha, but one time we were both sloppy drunk. I felt the condom that she had given me break, but the shit felt too good to stop. Plus, that was the last one in her stash. I should've known better. I had to lay low for a while because I heard her ugly ass was in a coma in the ICU. Like I said, this was just not my year.

∞

After Sha'Keisha burned me, I chilled the fuck out. I guess you could say that it scared the fuck out of me. A nigga decided to turn over a new leaf...so to speak. Since Alicia was being a bitch, I decided to make up with Tamar. I was practically living over her crib. It felt like we were a little family. It was nice being around my baby girl every day. She looked just like me.

She was a daddy's girl already. Every time I looked at her, I wondered about my seed that was still growing inside of Alicia. I wondered what Alicia looked like now. It had been months since I had last seen her. She was glowing and absolutely beautiful back then.

I wondered if she had that big ass nose that some chicks get during pregnancy. Did she have stretch marks now? Was she still having morning sickness? Did she have any weird cravings during the middle of the night? Were her feet fat and puffy? I felt terrible for missing out on all those things.

Imagine my surprise when I received a panicked phone call from Ms. Trina telling me that Alicia had been attacked and was in a coma. Then she told me that they had to perform an emergency C-section on her. To hear that my son was here and I had missed out on his birth because of these circumstances had me ready to blow up the city.

Who the fuck would've done this shit to my girl? Especially while she was carrying *my* seed. This was an automatic death sentence for all involved. I bet it was some local crackheads just trying to come up on a few bucks. Whoever it was had to be handled. I needed to talk to Alicia in order to get to the bottom of this shit. It was time to get my family back. All efforts had to be doubled!

« Chapter 4 Am I My Sister's Keeper? »

The Past "Eli"

"WHEW!!! SHIT! YOU SCANDALOUS bitches are trying to kill my ass in here today!" I yelled as I poured more baby oil into Kennedy's moms' asshole.

I showcased a huge smile as I watched Ms. Wet Pussy lapping at Gia's pussy like the good old bitch that she was. The visual was EVERYTHING! Satisfied with how lubricated her ass was, I plunged into her old ass without mercy. I roughly smacked her on her fat ass when I noticed her moaning into Gia's pussy, instead of licking it.

"Ms. Wet Pussy, I need you to keep eating that fat mutherfucka for me. I need that shit to be ready once I'm done playing in your tight ass. Now get to licking that pretty pink pussy!" I finished with another round of ass smacking.

She loudly moaned, but she did so into Gia's pussy as she licked it. Don't get me wrong, I absolutely loved pussy. However, these two broads were spoiling me with this unlimited butt fucking. I had been smashing the both of them for the past two months...as often as I could. I can't lie, I was addicted to this dynamic duo. They were down for whatever!

I even had them snorting coke off my dick before we all got to fucking. I still fucked Kennedy from time to time, however, her level of freaky just didn't compare to her mom's or best friend's. I gave my homeboy Country pointers on how to bag Kennedy's ass. Just like the disloyal bitch that I suspected she was, Country had that yellow ass bouncing like a low rider with hydraulics within minutes. Then she had the nerve to wonder why I never bothered wifing her up.

Country was the perfect distraction. He also made me feel less guilty about messing with the girl's mama and best friend. I felt that my actions were now justified. I fucked her mom and she fucked my homeboy. Every time I wanted to hit Ms. Wet Pussy and Gia, I would just call Country and tell him to make Ken disappear. It worked like a charm.

She had tried to cut shit off with Country a few times out of "loyalty" to me and because she felt guilty, but I'd just brush her off and deny her *The Dick* until she jumped back onto Country's.

Taking my dick out of Ms. Wet Pussy's gaping asshole, I removed my condom and straddled Gia's chest.

"You, open your mouth. And you, come over here and lick my ass while I get head from this bitch." I ordered the two of them.

Without uttering a word, both hoes complied. As I worked my dick in and out of Gia's mouth, Ms. Wet Pussy got to licking on my brown eye. I knew I couldn't last long. Before I knew it, I blew my load all the way down Gia's throat. She didn't waste a drop as she swallowed my precious seeds.

"Good girl! That shit is good for your skin, ma." I claimed with sincerity.

With my dick still rock hard, I mumbled, "Come ride this dick Gia. Ms. Wet Pussy, I'm craving pussy...come and sit on my face!"

In the mist of all this chaos, I had forgotten that I'd removed my condom until I was already deep inside of Gia. By that point, I said a quick prayer and continued to enjoy the gloveless ride!!! I loved being me!

∞

The next day, I had decided to do something extra special for Cee Cee. I had packed a picnic basket for us to indulge in on her lunch period. I didn't have any classes on Thursdays so I always tried to do something romantic for my girl. I had my grandmother make our food for this occasion. She had made her infamous fried chicken, macaroni and cheese, collard greens, candied yams, homemade rolls and pecan pie.

My grandmother dropped it all off warm and smelling delicious. Meeting Cee Cee in the hallway, I asked her to follow me. I told her that I had a surprise for her. She was so beautiful to me. So pure and innocent. She deserved a nigga much better than me. But I was always good to her in her presence.

She followed me outside to the tree where I'd left the basket. She looked at me puzzled and asked, "Eli, what's going on baby?"

"I brought us lunch. Help me lay this blanket down in the shade here. I hope you like everything." I replied.

"Awww! You never cease to amaze me boo! This is the sweetest thing ever! Whatever is in that basket smells heavenly! Let's eat!" She exclaimed rubbing her hands together.

I smirked at her little greedy ass. I don't know where she put it all. She could eat all day long, yet was still slim.

I opened the basket and we both went to work setting everything up. As I had predicted, my granny had put her foot into this meal. Cee Cee was so consumed with her food that she hadn't said much since we sat down. She was serious when it came to eating. Given her past, I understood why.

Grabbing her fork out of her hand, I started feeding her the pecan pie. She was even sexy when she pigged out on our feast. I loved catering to her. As I thought about our possibilities, I felt a stinging pain wash over my left cheek. Shocked by the sudden sensation, I jumped up to explore what the hell happened.

Swiftly spinning around, I saw Kennedy scowling at both me and Cee Cee. She appeared psychotic and I noticed that her hands were balled up.

"You stupid bitch! Did you just fucking slap me?!" I barked ready to murk this broad.

"Fuck you Eli! I've been loyal and running around in circles for your ass and you're over here catering to this dusty bum ass bitch?! Like for real??? I'd been hearing rumors, but I just refused to believe that you had stooped soooooo low! I had to see this fuckery with my own two eyes. This is where your 'interest lies'? I cannot believe you!!!" She distastefully spat.

"You've got to be kidding me, right? If you are so loyal, why is your skank ass letting my boy Country smash?! Get your scandalous ass the fuck outta here with that bullshit. Feed that load to a nigga that doesn't know any better bitch. You will never be shit to me! Don't disrespect my shorty either. She's never done shit to your jealous, hairy pussy having ass! Bounce bitch!" I dismissed her while chucking up the deuces.

I resumed feeding my baby who appeared unbothered by Kennedy's presence. At first Kennedy looked shocked and embarrassed. However, a sinister look soon washed over her scandalous face.

"It's okay muthafuckas, Country puts it down much better than you do in the bedroom. I'm done with your ass. Cee Cee, this means war for your raggedy ass too. You claim that she has never done shit to me, right? She has done everything to me. I blame her for everything that isn't right in my life. I curse the day she was ever born! Oh God, how I hate that little black bitch!" She screamed with a bewildered look in her eyes.

For the first time, Cee Cee peered at Ken with puzzlement etched on her face. She had even stopped eating.

Kennedy continued, "My life was amazing until your uppity mama came into the picture. You get to live the good life with our father. You're living in the nice house, in a nice neighborhood. You have the luxury of having both parents under one roof. I was once the apple of our father's eye. He stops by occasionally to drop off a few bucks or to fuck my mama. First you stole my daddy and now you've stolen my man.

I hate everything that you stand for and will see to it that you pay. Both of you bitches. By the way, I don't know how long you and Eli here have been fucking around, but I've been bouncing on that pus-colored dick for years. Actually, I just fucked him last week as a matter of fact. So tell me, how does my pussy taste, *sis*?" Ken taunted with a smug smirk on her face.

I absolutely hated that bitch. I couldn't believe that she was Cee Cee's sister. Another reason to hate her punk ass father! I could've put a bullet between Kennedy's eyes in that moment. I couldn't believe she had just revealed all that personal shit in front of all these nosy onlookers.

Her hatred towards Cee Cee now made all the sense in the world now. She wanted to be Cee Cee. I now knew that I not only had to protect Cee Cee from her parents, but now we both had to watch out for Ken's sneaky ass until I could cancel the bitch out. I was too afraid to look at Cee Cee's face, so I continued to shoot daggers at Ken.

"Oh damn Cee Cee, I almost forgot to tell you the most wonderful news of all!!!" She deviously squealed.

"Man Ken, get the fuck..." I attempted to say before Kennedy interrupted me.

"Guess what your man here did?! Give up? Your man here placed a bet that he could fuck you for a G within two weeks! Tsk Tsk Tsk. I know sis, I barely believed the shit myself when I heard it. At least they didn't bet your ass for some chump change...I guess." Kennedy shrugged.

"I just thought that I'd warn you little sis. No need to thank me of course. That's what big sisters are for!" She continued before bellowing out a hearty laugh.

I finally worked up enough courage to face Cee Cee. Silent tears were streaming down her devastated face. I didn't even know where to start, but I knew that I had to console her somehow.

"Listen Cee Cee, let's go somewhere and talk without an audience. Please don't listen to this jealous ass bitch. I swear to God, I had no idea that this hoe was your sister. Come here baby," I replied attempting to grab her arms to assist her into a standing position."

Cee Cee quickly pushed me away from her.

She finally spoke in a trembling voice, "Is what she said about the bet true?"

"Come on baby, let's not discuss that shit here." I replied.

"Tell me right here, right now Eli! Is it true?" She shouted.

"Yes and no. Yes, it all started off as a bet, but now what I feel for you is real. I swear it! I fucking love you girl! I could've been fucked you, collected the money and disappeared, but I didn't. I'm here! The more time that I spent with you, the more that shit began to feel foul. Please hear me out. Let's go somewhere private and talk." I pleaded.

"Eli, fuck you and this bitch! You love me, right? Yet you just fucked her a week ago. I am done with your trifling ass. Stay the hell away from me, you heartless bastard! I hate you!" She screamed.

She then started throwing the rest of the food at my ass. She dumped the rest of the candied yams over my head. She wildly threw drumsticks at my face and flung the collard greens all over my brand new Polo shirt. I just stood there and took it. I knew that she was pissed and embarrassed right now, but I knew that we could fix this.

I was just grateful that she didn't know about me fucking Ken's mama and best friend, Gia. I watched as Cee Cee took off towards her car. Looking over at Kennedy, I walked over to her laughing ass and two pieced that hoe to sleep. I instantly saw two knots forming on her forehead. I didn't believe in hitting women, however, this was not a woman at all. This bitch was a savage!

« Chapter 5 FML »

The Past "Celeste"

ALL I CAN SAY IS fuck my life! Why couldn't I seem to ever find my happy place. Just when I finally felt that things were going my way, the rug was roughly pulled from underneath me. Why did my fairytale have to vanish into thin air the way it had? My prince had suddenly morphed into a warty toad. I was humiliated incomprehensibly in front of many of my peers. I didn't know if I'd ever be able to face them again. As the saying goes, if it seems too good to be true then it probably is.

How could Eli have placed a bet on my virginity? I truly thought we were going somewhere. Before that dreadful day two weeks ago, I would have never considered his feelings for me to be anything less than genuine. I guess much like Mike, he deserved a standing ovation for his Academy Award winning performance. I had to give it to them...these niggas were good!

Out of all of the females at the party on my birthday, why was I singled out? Why didn't Eli's trifling ass bet on someone else? I hated his yellow ass! I'd been crying nonstop and isolating myself to my room when not at school, work or with Alicia and my new little nephew, Sincere. I hated that I missed him as badly as I did. What I missed the most was conversing with him every day. I missed the attention and affection that he showered me with.

I craved him more and more with each passing day. I saw him everywhere...although I knew deep down he wasn't truly there. This boy had me delusional and fiending for his ass. Nearly everything reminded me of him. I'd even caught myself resorting to smelling some of my items that still held his scent in them. The level of grief that I was experiencing by walking away from him was comparable to having lost him due to death. My heart could not differentiate between the two. A loss was a loss. The permanence of our situation was one and the same.

Two weeks ago, I was also blindsided by the news that Kennedy was my half-sister. To make matters worse, she was fucking my boyfriend. With that revelation, I couldn't have worked things out with Eli, even if I wanted to. While I'm playing Ms. Faithful to him, he is banging my sister! To be fair, I don't think he was aware that she was my sister, however, he was cognitively intact when he decided to slide his dick into someone else's twat.

This is exactly why bitches snap. Men love getting into our minds and having us thinking that we are special to them. They squirm their way into our hearts, knowing all they want is a piece of ass. Why work so hard for something your truly do not intend to cherish and enjoy for the long haul? What is the purpose? A nut? It just didn't seem worth the effort to me. Then again, I am speaking from a woman's point of view. I suppose some things are not meant for me to understand.

Strangely, Kennedy was able to bring me closure by revealing why she has tormented me from the first day she walked into my life. I can't believe that my parents never told me that I had a half-sister. Who hides shit like that?

I cannot count how many times I've came home crying as a result of something Kennedy had done to me. Her bullying and hatred for me was no secret, yet my parents never thought to tell me we were related. We've always attended the same schools, we were both bound to find out eventually.

In hindsight, I suppose the only person oblivious to the

secret sister, was me. She has obviously known since we were little girls. But why did she have to hate me? I didn't even know that she was family. I would have loved having a big sister growing up. She hated me for how my shitty parents treated her. Now I understood how she was able to attend my school, despite not living in the school district. I bet she used our address.

Internally I reminisced about how this bitch tormented me over the years. I'd come home crying, yet they'd never intervened. Apparently I was simply the punching bag for all misplaced anger. Alicia was the only friend that I had left aside from Shawn. She was shocked when she learned about everything that had transpired the day of the picnic. Without her, I would have crumbled, but she wasn't having any of that. We were TEAM FUCK MIKE & ELI!!!

∞

After our company gathering and meeting Joe's wife, I was more puzzled than ever. The look those two gave me that day as I walked to my car, made the hair on the back of my neck stand to attention. They were an odd pair. What the hell was their angle? For some odd reason, I had decided to remain at Divas R Us. After ripping up my transfer request, it was back to business as usual.

I loved my job and coworkers so the thought of leaving right now, was out of the question. Of course transferring to the other Divas R Us location was now out of the question as well. I couldn't work with Joe's wife every day. I just had to make sure to stay busy and to stay in well populated areas. I didn't trust Joe...or myself apparently.

Despite feeling awkward around Joe, I appreciated his willingness to ensure that Eli was not allowed on the premises. Security were to be notified immediately should he decide to enter the store. I didn't think that he would cause me any physical harm, I just wanted him to stay away from me. He knew better than to call my home number, but he'd called my work phone number and

Alicia relentlessly. He had also left numerous notes inside of my locker and on the windshield of my car.

I was having a difficult time as it was getting him off my mind. I wished he would just leave me alone. It was made crystal clear that he didn't give two shits about me, so why couldn't he just move on? Life was too short to waste pitying myself. I had almost lost my best friend...no...my sister over nothing. It made me question my own mortality. Missouri held nothing but terrible memories for me. Other than my friendship with Alicia, I had nothing going for me here. No one else gave a shit about me.

∞

One warm Sunday night after getting off an hour later than usual, I wearily walked to my car. Once reaching the spot where I was sure that I'd parked my beloved red beauty, I was at a loss. The parking lot was now fairly deserted. A few stragglers peppered the large parking lot, however, none of them came close to resembling my beauty.

I'm not sure if it was exhaustion or the shock of not seeing my car, but I was frozen in place. I continued to glance around subconsciously hoping that my BMW would magically reappear. Absentmindedly, I slowly trekked back to the mall. Once I reached Divas R Us, I loudly knocked on the glass hoping that Joe heard me.

Joe was the only person remaining in the store. He was most likely counting money and tying up other managerial loose ends. Moments after I started knocking an annoyed Joe emerged from the back of the store. Once realizing it was me, his face softened.

Unlocking the door he asked, "Hey Celeste, is everything

okay? I thought you were going home. Don't you have school in the morning?"

I instantly burst into tears. "Joe, someone stole my car! The buses have already stopped running for the day and I am stranded! What am I going to do?!"

"First things first, try to calm down sweetheart. It may not seem like it at the moment, but everything is going to be okay. You need to call the police and report the car stolen. Once that's taken care of, I will drop you off at home. Okay? Can I see a smile?" He consoled as he lifted my chin so that I'd have to look at him.

"You're absolutely right, thanks Joe." I responded with a weak smile.

After calling the police, we had to wait for about an hour for them to respond. They claimed that it was a busy night and this was a "nonemergent" matter. I prayed that my father had decided to stay out all night again. If he was at home and drinking, then I was screwed. After giving the officers all my information, the most talkative one named Officer Wayne gave me his business card. He promised to keep in touch.

Two hours after discovering that my car was missing, I was finally headed home. The store closed at seven on Sundays and it was now going on ten. I knew that I was going to have some explaining to do. My mom was okay with me staying over an hour later than originally scheduled, but I knew showing up three hours late was not good.

Joe and I rode in silence. I was too devastated to feign an interest in conversing with him. I appreciated the ride, but just wasn't up to talking. I was happy that he seemed to get the hint. Once pulling up to my house, I quickly thanked him for going above and beyond to help me. I know Alicia would have come to my rescue, but tomorrow was a school day and I didn't want her dragging her sisters and baby out this time of night.

As I prepared to get out of Joe's car, he gently grabbed my left wrist.

"Hold on Celeste. Can I talk to you for a minute? I know that it's late, so I won't keep you long. I just want you to know that I'm here for you. I mean it, I still consider you my *special friend* and refuse to see anything bad happen to you. I know things have been strained between us lately, but I'm happy that you've decided to stick it out. If they don't find your car within a few days, I'll take you to get another one.

I can't say that I'm not happy that Eli screwed up, but I hate to see you hurting like this. I want to see you back to your beautiful smiling self. Do you need me to pick you up from school tomorrow?"

"Thanks Joe, but I'll have Alicia drop me off tomorrow *if* they haven't found my car by then. I appreciate the kind words, but I couldn't accept a car from you. It was difficult enough taking one from Eli and we were dating. I'll manage somehow...I always do." I replied before saying goodnight and swiftly sliding out of the passenger seat.

Joe watched me until I was *unsafely* inside of my house. I beamed as I realized that all the lights were off. The house was eerily quiet as I slowly crept up each step, one at a time.

Thoughts of calling Eli tomorrow to inform him of the stolen car evaded my thoughts as I suddenly felt myself being harshly pushed backwards as I reached the top step. My tired body didn't stand a chance as I fought desperately to prevent my inevitable fall. All of my efforts to grab a hold of something to break my fall were all in vain.

I felt as if I were watching myself tumble down each step in slow motion. I recall the excruciating pain as my head slammed into at least two steps as I descended to the landing. My body landed with a loud thud. If I screamed on my way down, I do not remember it. I'd landed on my back with my left arm oddly tucked underneath me. That shit had to be broken! The angle was not normal.

I wondered why God had spared my life. I wished that fall had killed me. The room seemed to be spinning and I was pretty sure that I was suffering from a concussion.

Before blacking out from the pain, I heard a voice from the top of the stairs bellow, "I bet your grown ass won't come in late anymore, now will you? Get your fast ass up and get in the bed. I should've told the bitch to abort your whorish ass! The both of you disgust me!" A deep voice spat. He may have said more, but I can't recall because I had lost consciousness on that cold hardwood floor. Perhaps I'd imagined the voice altogether.

« Chapter 6 Truth Or Dare »

Present Day "Autumn"

"Please keep running,

And don't look back,

He's gonna catch you,

And throw you on your back,

You thought that you were grown,

And could handle any situation,

But now it's gonna take more than a prayer to God,

To get you out of this complication,

You wondered why when you told him that you loved him,

He didn't say it back,

Now you know the reason,

But it's too late,

You scream,

He gags,

You cry,

He laughs,

You fight,

He bites,

You question,

He ignores,

You told him that you weren't ready,

And he said that he understood,

But by the way that he was hurting you,

You were wondering how he could,

Whenever you cried,

He'd moan with so much pleasure,

As you screamed and gagged,

As he stole your treasure,"

I GLANCED AROUND AND shyly smiled as my classroom erupted into loud clapping and impressed praises. Up until that point, I'd held my breath not knowing how everyone would perceive my poem. With Mrs. Norwood's encouragement, I had made the decision to write about the touchy subject. She felt it was great.

While most of the class had opted to write about love, I had decided to write about the complete opposite...something real. That love shit wasn't real. You will never see me wasting my time writing about it. It took everything in me to stomach my classmates' false expectations. If only the poor dumb asses knew what I knew.

You tend to do better, when you know better. They'd see just how cold the big bad world is soon enough. As a kid, I knew early on that Santa Claus wasn't real, but I didn't ruin it for the ignorant. This was no different. No one would ever be able to accuse me of being a dream crusher.

Glancing at MaDonna, she held two thumbs and mouthed, "You go girl!"

We had become BFFs since working on our group project together. We got an A+ on that assignment too. I enjoyed spending time with her family probably as much as I liked hanging out with her. Her grandparents made me feel like I was one of their own grandchildren. You could feel the love as soon as you entered their home.

Their home was small, but tidy. It felt homey and welcoming. The Douglas's house was big and beautiful, but it never felt like home. I was always afraid of breaking something. It hardly looked lived in. Some might even refer to it as sterile.

Today, I was in an extremely good mood. Wintress was finally coming home tomorrow. The Prices' were going to meet Don tomorrow at a nearby park. We'd gain my sister and they'd be thirty-five thousand dollars richer. Perhaps they could use that money to continue fertility treatments or pay to adopt another kid. Wintress was simply out of the question.

It was Friday and Mrs. Douglas had agreed to allow MaDonna to stay over for the weekend. Of course, this meant that I wouldn't have to be bothered by the likes of Don for a couple of days. Besides when Wintress came home, I wanted all my favorite people to be with me. Don promised that as soon as he picked up Wintress, he was going to take us all to Six Flags for the day.

I had never been there before and was ecstatic! I felt like a child all over again. After school, I had our chauffeur take MaDonna and I shopping. We stopped by a chic yet affordable clothing store in the mall called Divas R Us. Although I had money now, you still wouldn't see me spending thousands of dollars on one outfit in a high-end store.

Don had given me eight hundred dollars the night before, just for the hell of it. I intended to spend every single cent on my

BFF and my sister. I didn't need anything because Don took care of everything for me. I told MaDonna to grab whatever she wanted.

I grabbed Wintress several outfits that I knew would look adorable on her. MaDonna tried on mostly dresses and they all looked amazing on her. Watching her dress and undress, I noticed that her undergarments were a little weathered. Both of her bra straps were being held in place by safety pins. I felt like such an ass in that moment. I had been giving her lots of clothes since we'd became friends, but it had never crossed my mind that she needed panties and bras as well.

Stepping out of the dressing room, I walked to the undergarments section. I had selected about five matching panty and bra sets. Divas R Us was also running a deal on their panties. They were selling ten panties for ten dollars. So, I decided to get her thirty panties in addition to her matching bra and panty sets. Now my home girl could go more than a month before having to repeat wearing her panties.

Before we were done, I had MaDonna get a couple of outfits for her siblings as well. Although it wasn't much, I hoped this lifted the burden off her grandparents just a little. Next time I'd grab them some items too. This store was very reasonable; however, eight hundred dollars only went so far.

After arriving home, MaDonna and I played board games with the boys. We all watched movies and pigged out on junk. Mrs. Douglas had ordered us pizzas and wings from Imo's Pizza. This was a rarity. She'd always insisted on cooking for us every day. Eventually Chris and Landon checked out on us so MaDonna and I went to my room. She was the first to jump into the shower and take care of her nightly hygiene.

I had snuck a little alcohol from Mrs. Douglas' bar area. After all, what was a sleep over without a little alcohol? Once she finished in the bathroom I followed suit. I cleansed myself with my favorite Dove body wash. Once I finished showering, I brushed my teeth and wrapped my hair up for the night. Walking back into my bedroom, I peeped MaDonna watching My 600-lb Life on the tv.

"Bitch, how can you stomach this shit? Those big muthafuckas make me want to have my mouth sewn shut!" I joked.

"I don't know. I just love this show for some reason. I always pray that they can stick to their proposed diets and lose the weight before it's too late. I feel so sorry for them. Most of them have had traumatic childhoods. They pack on all those pounds to protect themselves. Eating is their coping mechanism. They hope that it will keep people from continuing to harm them only to find out that it makes them targets for other reasons." MaDonna replied.

"Wow, you talk as if you're speaking from experience." I said.

"I suppose I am...in a way. I was a chubby kid and was bullied and teased about it. Luckily for me, that torment had the opposite effect on me. I didn't want to be fat forever. You know?" She revealed.

"I feel you there girl. Well you are gorgeous just the way you are best friend!" I squealed jumping up to dance without music.

As I twerked in her face, she threw a pillow at me and we burst into a fit of laughter. I loved seeing her this way. Happiness made her glow and she was prettier than ever.

"Girl, let's play truth or dare. Every time either of us refuses to answer a question, we have to take a shot to the head." I suggested.

"Cool, I'm game." She agreed.

"Home court advantage...me first!" I gloated.

"Heifer, we are ten seconds into the game and you are already cheating. Go ahead!" She huffed jokingly.

"Whatever! Truth or dare?" I asked.

"Ummm truth." MaDonna replied.

"Is it true that you are feeling Darius Bryson? Girl I be peeping you checking him out!" I teased.

"Autumn, hell no! Not even close! He is most certainly not my type. Try again boo!" She laughed dismissively.

"Now, my turn crazy woman," she continued. "Truth or dare, Roe?" She asked calling me by the nickname she'd adopted from my last name.

"Truth!"

"Is it true that you still have your *V card?*" She inquired.

I shook my head sadly before replying, "Unfortunately, not anymore. I'd give almost anything to be able to say that I did. What about you?"

"Cheating again, aren't we? I didn't select truth!" She pointed out.

I sighed, "Truth or dare?"

"Dare."

"Well I dare your black ass to answer the question that I just asked you!"

"How about I don't and plead the fifth bitch!" She laughed.

"Suit yourself best friend, but be prepared to chug-a-lug," I shrugged.

I'm not scurrrrred of a little alcohol. Give it here!" She demanded as she playfully snatched the bottle out of my hands.

I sat back and watched as she took that shot straight to the dome. I must admit, I was impressed. I'd never drank before and I knew it wouldn't be easy going down. If it tasted the way that it smelled, I knew that it would be coming right back up!

Wiping off her mouth with the back of her hand, she smirked at me and replied, "Truth or dare Roe?"

"Dare."

"I dare you to twerk upside down on a handstand." She replied, her golden orbs dancing under the light.

"Bitch that is too easy! You know that I'm a dancing machine!"

With that, I hiked my nightgown up and gracefully summersaulted into an upside down position. Spinning around on my hands to face my friend, I seductively licked my lips as I took notice of her shocked expression to my unclad body. Don never allowed me to wear panties or bras under my nightgowns so with me being upside down, my entire bare body was exposed.

I slowly begin to twerk to an imaginary beat. I made sure to hypnotize her as I isolated each of my ass cheeks in a rhythmic beat. Picking up the momentum, the sounds of my plump ass cheeks clapping together echoed throughout my large room.

Once I was sure that I'd adequately fulfilled my dare, I swiftly dropped down into a split ensuring that my ass jiggled on impact.

"Truth or dare?" I asked.

"How the fuck am I supposed to top that shit bitch?!" She exclaimed.

"Girl, you are so silly! I'd rather do almost anything not to drink that nasty ass shit!" I stated seriously pointing at the bottle of Vodka.

"Now stop stalling, truth or dare?" I repeated.

"Truth again!" She giggled.

"I'm about tired of your safe ass and all these damn truths bitch! Is it true that you liked watching this pussy pop with no hands? I saw you over there drooling!" I said putting her on the spot.

I watched her blush and squirm in her seat before replying, "Roe, I'm not even going to dignify that shit with a response."

"Unfortunately for you, that response is along the same lines as pleading the fifth. Gets 'tuh' drinking!!!" I demanded.

"With pleasure," she replied downing her second shot.

MaDonna and I played the game for another twenty minutes or so. In that time, she had to down two more shots for not answering my questions. Believe it or not, I actually had to down one. MaDonna was toasty and was dozing off. I didn't want her to sleep on the floor so I physically had to help her into my bed. She was small in stature so it wasn't too difficult of a task to do.

While helping her, I noticed for the first time how soft she was. She also smelled amazing...just like my Dove body wash and Versace perfume. The way that she landed on my bed had her short nightgown hiked up around her waist. Like me, she wasn't wearing any panties.

She looked so beautiful laying there lightly snoring. I felt so conflicted as I stood there watching her neatly trimmed bush glistened with her juices. I had never wanted to taste anything more in my entire life. I was literally salivating. Stirring in her sleep, each of her legs fell to the side giving me the perfect view of her moist center.

What was I to do? Take advantage of my intoxicated best friend or take my ass to sleep? Being the curious person that I am, I decided to raise her nightgown above her breasts. They were so perfect. The contrast between her caramel complexion and her dark chocolate nipples was so alluring. I decided to throw caution to the wind. I wanted her so badly that I was willing to jeopardize our friendship.

Leaning down, I popped one of her erect nipples into my mouth. As I nibbled on one, I made sure to tweak the other with my fingers. Although asleep, she moaned lightly as her body responded to my touch. I bathed her with my tongue as I suckled on her poised neck. It all felt so wrong, yet so right as my silky tongue snaked its way down her abdomen and landed just above her mound.

I felt like a kid in a toy store. I didn't know what I wanted to play with first. Wrapping my forearms around MaDonna's luscious thighs, I gently pulled her to the end of my bed. Before feasting on her seductive center, I just stared at it for a few moments taking in her scent and memorizing the way her pearl peeked at me.

Not able to wait any longer, my mouth applied a soft suction to her clit. MaDonna's body stiffened and I noticed changes in her breathing pattern. I wondered if she thought she was dreaming. Her eyes never opened. As I flicked my tongue up and down her pink slit, I heard her hissing as she pushed on my head. Her legs were clamped tightly around my head as she expelled a copious amount of her cum into my mouth. How in the hell do you cum in your sleep?!

She tasted so delicious and I knew I wouldn't be brushing her off my tongue tonight. I wasn't done with her just yet. I pulled her up to the top of my bed and positioned my pussy above hers. My pussy was just as wet as hers as our bodies connected. As I rocked back and forth rubbing clit upon clit, all that was heard in my room was what sounded like macaroni being stirred. The soundtrack in this room was amazing.

After we tribbed for a few minutes, I released a flood of my very own fresh pussy juices down onto hers. Exhausted and feeling the effects of the shot that I'd consumed, I was ready to call it a night. I planted one final kiss onto MaDonna's soft bush before fixing her gown. I toyed with the thought of wiping off her wet pussy, however, I loved the thought of her wearing my juices tonight. I wondered if she'd notice in the morning.

Laying down beside MaDonna, I wanted to snuggle next to her. I fought the urge. What did all of this mean? Should I tell her what we did? What I did? Would she be upset? Disgusted?

Creeped out? I concluded that she shouldn't know. I'd never bring it up. I was a little embarrassed, but I'd do it all again if the opportunity presented itself. What if Don found out somehow? He made it clear that I was never to be touched by anyone. I'm sure that included my best friend.

Did this mean that I was gay? I had never been attracted to another woman before, but I couldn't seem to fight these feelings for MaDonna. I felt this strange chemistry between she and I from the first time we met. I had never felt these feelings, these urges for anyone else...man or woman. I drifted off to sleep wondering if MaDonna was capable of ever having similar feelings for me. I knew that I was in love with her and would stop at nothing to make her mine.

« Chapter 7 The Mourning After »

Present Day "Autumn"

THE NEXT MORNING, I rolled over and noticed that MaDonna was no longer beside me. Panicked, I leaped out of bed and sped towards the bathroom. My heart sank once I realized she wasn't in there either. Jetting down the stairs while calling her name, I stopped in my tracks upon seeing her making breakfast in the kitchen. The boys were sitting on the stools in front of the kitchen island watching cartoons.

"Good morning Sleeping Beauty! We thought you were going to sleep the day away." She smiled.

"Good morning everyone. Wh...what time is it Donna?"

"It's going on eleven. You looked so peaceful that I couldn't bear to wake you. Did you know that you fart in your sleep?" She asked as both of my little brothers fell over laughing.

"I do not! Forget all three of you!" I shot back blushing.

"Where's Mrs. Douglas and Don?" I inquired looking around.

"First of all, yes you do. And she came in the room early this morning saying that her sister had a stroke so she had to catch the next flight to Boston. I was coming back from the bathroom when she came in. I told her that I'd relay the message once you woke up. I told her that you'd gone to bed late. I'm not sure where Don went to." She elaborated.

"Oh no! A stroke! I hope everything is okay!" I shouted.

"Calm down Roe, Mrs. Douglas said that she'd call as soon as she touched down and had an update. Here, sit down. I made you some breakfast too. You came just in time. These two little boogers tried to smash your food while you were asleep." MaDonna consoled.

"Thanks, best friend. You're the best! I could eat a horse right about now." I replied seriously.

Landon signed asking if he and Chris could play video games in our entertainment room. I told them that I was okay with it as long as their room was clean. They both quickly nodded and darted in the direction of the entertainment room. I shook my head at the both of them. They were inseparable.

When they first moved here, they each had their own rooms, but after a week of trying to get them to stay in their own rooms, Mrs. Douglas finally gave up. She moved all of Chris's belongings into Landon's room since he had the bigger room.

I was snapped out of my thoughts as MaDonna's leg brushed up against mine as she sat next to me. Damn this was awkward. I couldn't even look her in the eyes.

"Donna, how on Earth are you up and functioning right now? You drank all those shots, yet, you are running around here like Suzie Homemaker. I only had one shot and I feel like a corpse."

"Autumn that wasn't shit. It just gave me a nice little buzz and made me sleepy. Believe me when I say, I was awake and alert through everything last night." She stated with a seductive smirk.

I could feel my cheeks growing flushed from humiliation.

"No need to be embarrassed. Nothing happened, that I

didn't want to happen. Roe, I'm gay and I have always been attracted to you. My gaydar could sense that you were curious. To answer your questions from last night, no I'm not a virgin. I've dated quite a few guys before I concluded that I was definitely gay. I couldn't pretend anymore.

Yes, you definitely turned me on with your upside down twerking moves. I've always wanted to tell you that I was in to you, but I didn't want to ruin our friendship and chase you off." She confessed.

I was at a loss for words. I couldn't believe that she had been awake the entire time.

As if reading my mind, she continued, "Autumn, I highly doubt that even the drunkest chick could remain asleep while getting ate out. If she could, I'm scared of that hoe!" She chuckled.

Although she had put me on the spot, she still made me feel at ease about the entire ordeal. Was I gay like her? I didn't think so because she was the only female that I was attracted to sexually and I thought lots of guys were sexy.

"Why didn't you let me know that you were awake?" I asked.

"I don't know. I guess, I didn't want to frighten you and make you chicken out. Was this your first time being with a woman?"

I nodded and looked down into my sweaty palms. What was she doing to me?!

"I honestly didn't know what I was doing Donna. I just had these overwhelming urges and no matter how hard I tried, I couldn't ignore them. It's all so complicated. Was I your first girl?"

"No, but I wish you were. My first was an older woman. I actually met her online. She promised to teach me everything that she knew. I guess she taught me too well because her crazy ass soon wanted to leave her husband of fifteen years for me. I didn't love her and didn't want to be with her at all. I just wanted to learn how to be an amazing lover.

She didn't know how to let go. I was close to getting a restraining order and filing statutory rape charges against her ass. She finally fell back once she realized that I was dead serious. The bitch was bold enough to show up at school and slide under the bathroom stall to talk to me. I couldn't deal with that nutty old broad anymore.

The other girl was our age. I liked her a lot, but she was too butch for me. If you'd looked in the dictionary under the word dike, you'd find her picture. I wasn't ready to be out like that. She had no discretion what so ever. I'm a private person and my business isn't everyone's business. I'm not embarrassed by my sexuality, I just don't believe in flaunting the shit. The people who need to know, already do." She elaborated.

"So, what do you like about me Donna?"

"What isn't..."

Before she could finish, the front door loudly swung open. In walked a raging mad, battered Don. He appeared as if he'd been crying or something. Blood was dripping from his head, but it was hard to pinpoint where from. He was talking incoherently. In trying to make out what he was mumbling, all I gathered was money, stole, baby.

"Money...stole...baby! Money...stole...baby!" Don continued to repeat over and over again.

"Don, what's wrong! Please talk to me, you aren't making

any sense. Please, you're scaring us. Did something happen to your aunt in Boston?!"

The boys were both clinging to me in tears. MaDonna looked on at Don's bizarre meltdown. I didn't know what else to do so I decided to show Don a little compassion. I wrapped my arms around him, hoping that he would soon snap out of his irrational frame of mind. I had to ignore Donna's questioning eyes at the moment. I knew that at some point I'd have to explain my actions, but right now, we were facing a crisis.

Whispering in his ear I said, "Tell me what's wrong daddy. What happened to you out there baby?"

My soft words seemed to relax Don a little. I felt the tension leave his body.

Stepping backwards out of my embrace, he blinked several times while focusing on my face. I could see the recognition return to them.

He began to cry uncontrollably before saying, "Oh Autumn, I'm such a fuck up. Everything that I touch turns to shit!"

We looked on as he punched several holes into the expensive walls.

He continued, "I wanted to surprise you. I left early so that I could pick up Wintress before you woke up today. When I arrived, I was pistol whipped. Those thieving animals took my $35,000 and they took off with my fucking daughter!!!"

In that moment you could've heard a pen drop. That alcohol had me hearing things. I couldn't have heard him correctly.

Shocked by his words, in a shaky voice I asked Don to repeat himself. I needed reassurance.

"Autumn you fucking heard me right! I told you once before that you coming here was no accident. Wintress is my daughter and they took her!!!"

\

« Chapter 8 Diamond In A Rough »

The Past "Lukas"

AFTER GLADYS HAD DECIDED that she could no longer associate herself with a drug dealing pimp, a nigga was hurt. I'd never admit it to her, but I felt some kind of way about her decision. I thought about reaching out several times, however, my pride just wouldn't allow me to. She was a good girl and she deserved a good man. I fell back and told myself that when I finally came back for her, I'd come correct.

I threw myself into my work. It was a nice distraction from G. I'd driven past her house several times, but a neighbor told me that she moved on campus. She only stopped by her house once or twice a week now.

My homeboy Reese called requesting that I come down to Dallas to help him capture some women to be sold across seas. This meant major stacks for the both of us. I had to slow down my movements in the Lou because the missing posters were getting out of control. Naturally I agreed to his generous offer. He knew that I was the best in the game and was bound to catch lots of bad bitches slipping.

I appreciated the change in scenery. I had been to D-Town before, but I didn't remember the women being this beautiful. They were running circles around those St. Louis broads...much thicker too. Those broads had to be eating their cabbage and cornbread! I rubbed my hands together as I glanced around and saw nothing but dollars signs with fat asses bouncing around. Nothing made my dick rock up faster than a bowlegged, pigeon toed country girl.

I told Reese that I wanted to get to work as soon as my plane touched down. I brought two of my main hoes with me, Thandie and Paige. I figured they could also help bring in some unsuspecting bitches. Who better than to recruit a hoe, then a fellow hoe, ya dig? The way that I operated was simple...always quality over quantity. Many of these fake as pimps failed in the business because they were under the misconception that more was best.

I had learned long ago that I could quadruple my earnings by focusing on the diamonds in the rough. How much could a nigga expect to earn by selling basic run down bitches? They had no value in this business. The big money buyers wanted the virgins, the innocent, wholesome girls, wifey material...beauty definitely didn't hurt either. Naturally, underage girls brought in the biggest profit. What a wealthy pedophile wouldn't pay for one of them!

Don't get me wrong. Money was money. I would have my girls run game on and bring even the basic hoes to me, but I never had high expectations. Also, I'd never devote my personal time reeling them in. I was an important guy and didn't have time for insignificant bitches.

None of this shit even bothered me. I was desensitized to it all. I didn't know anything else, but this life. I thought this shit was normal. The only time I felt any remorse about my actions was when I thought about how I had planned to force G into this world. I just couldn't introduce her to this life even if it meant I took a huge L. I wanted her for myself. She was *my* diamond in the rough.

I vowed to enroll into St. Louis Community College - Forest Park campus once I got back home. A degree in business would help me tremendously when it came to starting up my own legitimate business one day. For now, I needed to focus on catching some girls. Tonight, we were all going to an art gallery. We'd all split up and see if we could each catch a fish.

∞

I stood in the mirror decked out in a custom made black Armani tux, gold cuff links and black Ferragamos. My favorite 18K Presidential Rolex watch adorned my left wrist. My curly hair was cut extremely low, just the way I liked it. I left it long enough just to make the ladies lust and wish I'd give them some curly haired babies. I looked and smelled like a million bucks.

I made sure my money clip was fat. I'd have to do some showboating and cash flashing tonight as bait. Pulling up in the all black stretch limo, I popped a mint into my mouth. I was feeling lucky tonight. I was going to catch a big fish. The big fish would make me twenty-five to fifty thousand dollars...easily.

The basic bitches only brought in five to ten thousand dollars. So please understand why I'd rather catch one good one, instead of several mediocre bitches.

Thoroughly inspecting the stock on the floor, I didn't see anyone that tickled my fancy. The night was still young so I decided to be the patient guy that I was and ordered me a glass of red wine. I mingled with the other stuffy patrons while attempting to appear interested in the wack ass art displays.

A lot of this shit was just weird. I'm sure they all had their own hidden stories behind them, however, none of them appeared worth the outrageous price tags attached to them. While some definitely took a lot of time to complete, others looked like a first-grader's handiwork. I couldn't believe that it was even legal to sell some of that ugly ass shit!

As I continued to walk around and feign interest in the abstract painting section, I heard the most seductive feminine voice ever. What was so intriguing about that voice was that its owner was most certainly not a Texan. No, in fact, she was a fellow St. Louisan.

Slowly turning around, I was graced by the sight of one of the most beautiful women that I had ever seen. She was elegantly dressed and I could tell that she either came from money or had a very generous sponsor. Although, I knew she was from my home turf, I'd never seen her before. How had we coexisted in the same state, yet never bumped into each other before?

I discreetly watched her as she admired painting after painting. I wanted to walk up to her, yet, I didn't know shit about art. I feared that she would quiz me on the paintings and make me look like an ass. Just as I had worked up enough nerve to approach this mocha colored beauty, I noticed a very familiar nigga swoop in and embrace her.

Stopping in my tracks, I decided to stand back and monitor their exchange. What was the extent of their relationship exactly? How could I get her away from his ass? That bitch was a guaranteed pay day, but I didn't think that I'd be able to snag her tonight with Big E's cock blocking ass standing there. They appeared to be in a relationship and were all over each other.

I can't explain it, but I was green as fuck as I watched him interact with her. I didn't even know the bitch, but I was ready to pistol whip her nigga for being too close to her. I could tell that he was just as enamored by her lovely charm as I was. She pointed at two paintings totaling over twenty-seven thousand dollars and he quickly saw to it that she got them.

Who was this bitch?! I knew Big E from around the way. We weren't friends nor had we ever conducted any business together, but he'd made a decent name out in the streets for himself. He was the plug and supplied most of south St. Louis and east St. Louis with their work. I had nothing but respect for the nigga, to be perfectly honest.

He was definitely older than me and little momma. He had

to be in his late thirties. She appeared to be a little older than Gladys. I continued to watch the both of them while ensuring that I wasn't detected by Big E. Ms. Mocha squealed and jumped on Big E to show her appreciation for her newly acquired paintings. With her legs wrapped snuggly around him, I couldn't help but to notice that she had those sexy ass dimples on her lower back.

I don't know what it was about back dimples, but that shit drove me crazy! Licking my pink lips, I envisioned the day that I'd be able to dip my tongue into them muthafuckas. I'd definitely have to sample that ass before I made a fortune off of her. She was definitely a *diamond*. Watching the giddy duo leave with their overpriced paintings in tow, I knew that I'd have to research Big E in order to find out who that bitch was. I had to find her ass back in the Lou and line my pockets off her sale.

Not too long after Ms. Mocha left, I felt a warm pair of arms wrap around my chest.

"Damn big daddy, are you going to let me see if all the stereotypes about black dicks is true?" The voice asked.

Looking down at the hands, I noticed three things about them. One, they belonged to a white broad. Two, the bitch was married. Neither of which meant a thing to me. Of course, a married bitch's disappearance would be noticed and reported faster, however, she'd never be found where she was going. Three, judging by the size of her ring, her ass was seriously caked up.

Smiling as I slowly spun around, I was a little disappointed by the mediocrity of the basic bitch before me. I knew that I had to conduct a serious sales pitch in order to unload her ass. Don't get me wrong, the bitch was no slouch in the looks department...she was very pretty.

She just simply wasn't on diamond status like Mocha. Most of our buyers tended to like exotic, foreign and black women anyway. If I was lucky, I could probably get about nine thousand dollars for her. Always one to find the bright side of things, I took solace in the fact that her ring alone was worth more than her ass was, on the market. I'd easily get thirty thousand back for that huge rock. Peering into her sea green eyes, I took her small hand into mine as I led her towards her new life.

« Chapter 9 X Marks The Spot »

The Past "Alicia"

YESTERDAY WAS ONE OF the best days of my life. Sincere was finally medically cleared and discharged from the hospital a little over a month after his original due date. Nothing could have prepared me for caring for a sick baby. Leaving my son in the NICU was one of the most difficult things that I've ever had to do. How could I celebrate finally going home without my son accompanying me in the back seat?

I knew it was necessary and he had to get stronger, but I hated visiting only to leave him every day. Most of my days were spent up there holding, singing and feeding my baby. I didn't want him to forget who I was. Cee Cee, my mother and Mike were also mainstays in the hospital.

Although I initially tried to avoid Mike, I knew it was impossible to dodge him while our son was hospitalized. Most days we'd sit and interact with Sincere while not saying anything to one another. He tried to initiate several awkward conversations, but I always deaded that shit. If it wasn't about our son...I was not interested. At some point I knew that we'd have to discuss the whole Tamar situation, but that was not my top priority at the moment. I'd fill him in when the time was right.

He'd get me food from the cafeteria or coffee from the nourishment room. However, being the petty bitch that I am, I'd swiftly trash that shit right in front of his ass. Fuck Mike! After all he's done to me, we'd never be cool. I didn't want shit from him.

The only thing he needed to focus on was Sincere and his other baby. I was through.

Having Sincere home was a blessing. I finally began to feel like a normal mom. My baby no longer had tubes and monitors connected to his little body. I didn't have nosey ass nurses watching me interact with my son as if I was a second-class citizen when it came to caring for him. My sisters were so helpful and protective over their nephew. They were not allowed to see much of him while he was in the hospital due to the strict age restrictions.

Mike's family were very involved too. His parents stopped by all the time to spend time with their grandson. They'd wanted to take him out several times, but I wasn't ready for that. I was only comfortable with my mom leaving with him without me being present. Maybe in time when Sincere was a little older, his dad and paternal grandparents could take him out.

About two months after Sincere was discharged home, I decided to take him out for some fresh air. I hadn't really felt comfortable leaving the house a lot since the attack. My mother felt that I should see someone because she was convinced that I was suffering from PTSD. I had the most vivid yet horrific dreams that often caused me to wake up screaming on several occasions. I'd wake my entire household up in a panicked frenzy.

I'll be honest, Tamar and Shay had me a little spooked. I prayed that nothing popped off while I had my son with me. If my pregnant belly wasn't sufficient enough to stop her brutal attack, I knew Sincere's physical presence wouldn't be either. I grabbed a sharp razor blade and some pepper spray just to air on the side of caution.

Glancing in the mirror near the front door, I became saddened by everything I had lost this year...especially after the attack. I had missed out on a lot of my junior year. I had become pregnant, contracted a venereal disease, found out that my man was unfaithful and had been with at least two other women. One of which he had fathered another child with. I had been physically and verbally attacked by the man that I was sure was destined to be my husband one day.

My son had been practically beat, shot and stomped out of me. I had to parent him from a hospital while also recovering myself physically and mentally. His father's daily presence constantly reminded me of how much he'd fucked up my life.

My right cheek was permanently scarred by Tamar's jealous act. While the surgeon had worked a miracle and was hopeful that the laceration would completely disappear in time, I wasn't so sure. Since she had pulled out and cut a lot of my hair, I had my beautician cut it into a short layered style.

Looking back, I looked a lot like Grace Byers from Empire...only I was more beautiful. It was a bit of an adjustment. I was still self-conscious about the new haircut and cut on my face. I couldn't even hide it with my hair, because it was now so short. Ensuring I had my son's supplies, I picked up his car seat and headed for the door.

I had decided to take my boy to the St. Louis Zoo before it got too warm out. I knew that he was too young to really enjoy the beauty of the animals, but it had always been one of my favorite places to go...even now. I'd bought several kodak disposable cameras and captured some beautiful shots of Sincere and the animals. He seemed to be enjoying his little self. I would have invited the twins and Cee Cee but they were all busy. The twins were attending a week long cheerleading camp and Cee Cee was at work.

For now, it was just me and my little guy. We left after two hours. I decided that we could use a few things from Wal-Mart, so I drove us to the supercenter on Highway 67. I secured my son's car seat in the shopping cart and wandered aimlessly down the aisles.

I grabbed things that I felt we needed, but most of the items we did not. I grabbed some toys for my son and little sisters. I grabbed some new CDs that I'd been wanting to get for a while. By the time, we made it to the checkout line, my total had come to seven hundred and twelve dollars.

"Dang son, your Nana is going to get you for spending all of that money." I jokingly cooed to my bright eyed little boy as I dug into his baby bag to retrieve my wallet.

"I got that." I heard a deep voice speak, but didn't pay much attention to it as I finally spotted my Gucci wallet.

Grabbing the credit card that my mother permitted me to use, I handed it to the cashier with a smile. The cashier looked at me with a puzzled look before replying, "Miss, the gentleman behind you has already paid for your items." He pointed at the guy standing behind me.

Turning around to address the generous guy, I was taken back by how unattractive he was.

"Sir, I thank you, but that really wasn't necessary. There is an ATM over there, so that I can give you your money back. But again, I appreciate your thoughtfulness." I kindly smiled at the hideous stranger.

He appeared unaffected as he replied, "No problem. I'll meet you over there once I finish up here."

I didn't want him paying for my things, however I was a slightly annoyed that he didn't insist that I keep the money just a little. Plus, now I had to wait for his ugly ass to finish up before I could leave. I was growing hungry and crabby. His little act of kindness was turning into an inconvenience. I waited by the ATM for this guy for approximately five minutes because he'd also went crazy down the aisles apparently. As he approached me, I handed him five hundred dollars.

He counted the bills and asked, "Where's the rest of it?"

"Oh sorry, I can only withdraw five hundred dollars a day from my card. If you follow me to the bank, I can see if I can get them to release more." I stated annoyed by the entire ordeal.

The nerve of this nigga to count the money and question me! No one told his monkey ass to pay for my shit to begin with!

"Sorry Miss, I have somewhere I have to get to after I leave here. Here, take my card and give me a call when you are able to get the rest of the money. No rush." He replied.

"Okay, I will be able to get the rest of your money tomorrow. I'll call you as soon as I do...Mr. Cartwright." I assured, looking at his business card. I had noticed that since my attack I had a tendency to try to hide the cut on my face by angling my head a particular way. His intense stare made me very uneasy and I was doing my best to hide my laceration.

"Please, just call me Noel. My father is Mr. Cartwright."

"Well then...*Noel*, I have to get going. I have to tend to my son. Expect a call from me sometime tomorrow to take care of this matter." I replied no longer able to contain my annoyance.

"No worries. Go ahead and get little man together. I'll talk to you tomorrow," he replied smiling down at my son.

"Sounds like a plan. Goodbye now." I yelled back at him, switching my ass up out of that Wal-Mart.

I could feel him staring at my ample bottom as I strutted through the exit. I knew I wasn't perfect and had flaws of my own, but his busted ass didn't stand a chance with a chick like me. I had to give it to him though; he was dressed to the nines and smelled amazing.

He carried himself as if he was someone extremely important. I don't think he realized that he was unattractive either. He exuded nothing but confidence and that kind of turned me on...for a very brief moment. Truthfully, none of that shit even mattered; he was just too ugly to be seen in public with. I'm not shallow or anything, but he was just too grotesque to take seriously.

Politely put, he resembled a gorilla. He was very fit and he appeared to live in the gym but...his face...his lips...his nose...all left me speechless, but not in a good way. As I drove out of the parking lot, I thought about how I was going to pay him his money and be done with that fuck face for good!

∞

Later that day, I was sleeping in my bed when I felt my bed shift. Thinking I was dreaming, I ignored it. Feeling my covers being pulled off me caused me to quickly sit up. Wiping the sleep from my eyes, I was pissed when I noticed none other than Mike sitting on my bed.

"Baby, we need to talk." He appeared to be under the influence of something.

"Mike, how in the hell did you get in here?!" I shrieked, but not loud enough to wake up our son.

"Girl, do you seriously think those weak ass locks y'all have could keep me out? I would've broken in sooner, but I called myself giving you time to think. Well baby mama...your time is up! I'm sick of shit the way it is. I miss you and I hate not coming home to you and Sincere every day. I've apologized a million times already.

I'm sorry for everything. Can you please take me back? I promise you won't regret that shit. Please baby please! Stop being mad at me okay? Let daddy come home. It's over between me and Tamar...and all the other women. Look me in the eyes and tell me you don't miss a nigga," He replied glaring at me lustfully.

"No Mike, I don't miss that shit. I'm over it, so please leave now."

"Look me in the eyes and say that shit Alicia!" He insisted.

Looking him in his eyes, I replied, "Like I said, what we had is over. I've moved on and I suggest you do the same. Get out and don't sneak your cheating black ass back into my crib again."

"Bitch what the fuck you mean you've moved the fuck on?! You fucking some other nigga? You have these lame ass niggas around my muthafucking seed?" He barked while delivering a series of stinging slaps to my cheeks.

Our son instantly woke up and belted out a surprised cry. Hopping out of my bed to console my upset son, Mike grabbed and body slammed me onto the bed.

"Your ass is out here being a hoe and giving *my* pussy away?! Is that why your funky ass got your hair cut like that? You out here looking good for your *new* nigga?! Bitch, you are about to learn today!"

"Mike stop! I haven't been fucking anyone else! I swear I haven't. Let's talk about this rationally. You're scaring Sincere. Don't do this to me in front of our baby Mike! I thought you were sorry!" I cried as he ripped my panties from my body.

I don't think my words even reached him. My son was still screaming at the top of his lungs as Mike turned me onto my stomach. He then pinned my arms down above my head and roughly entered my body. I felt as if I were being ripped into two. I had been with Mike many times, but my body was not prepared for this. I cried into my pillow because of the pain as well as the powerlessness I felt at the moment.

I was pissed because I was being deprived of the ability to calm my terrified son down.

"Unhhhh Alicia! God damn girl! I've missed the fuck out of this tight ass pussy! Sssssss...fuck baby!!! You are going to fuck around and make me put another one in your ass!" He bellowed as he rapidly stroked in and out of my sore pussy.

"Alicia, I love you so much! You'll never leave me, you do know that right? Sure, you may think that you hate me now because of my approach. But please realize that I just want my family back...this shit is all out of love," he grunted as he continued to pound away at me from behind.

"Fuck...fuck...fuck! I'm almost there, baby. Are you ready to get knocked up again? Hunh?!" He said picking up his pace.

I could tell by his strokes that he was just a few thrusts away from cumming inside of me. I had to intervene somehow.

Thinking quickly, I yelled, "Mike, stop! I have to tell you something!"

His thrusts instantly came to a halt.

"Tamar and her home girl Shay...I think her name was are the ones who attacked me when I was pregnant with Sincere! Kill those bitches for me and our baby...then we can be a family!"

Pulling out of me and turning me onto my back, I could see death written all over his handsome face. "Are you absolutely sure it was them?" He asked.

"I've never been more sure of anything in my entire life Mike. She tried to kill us both. I don't feel safe out there with her roaming around. Take care of her...for us." I pleaded, internally pleased that my tactic had worked.

"Oh, those bitches are beyond dead Alicia! I already told you what time it was for all parties involved in that shit." He stated walking over and picking up our furious son.

I wanted nothing but to shoot Mike and snatch my baby away from him. Sincere calmed down almost instantly as his naked ass rapist father gently rocked him back to sleep.

Laying a sleeping Sincere back into his bassinet, Mike replied, "Consider those hoes handled baby. I got you. Oh yeah, I wasn't able to get that last nut off because of the interruption, but I already came in you three times baby mama." He gloated while motioning to my gaping pussy as it oozed his sticky seeds.

I had been so consumed by all this madness, that I hadn't even noticed this shit.

"I hadn't fucked you in so long, therefore each time I nutted my dick was still hard as fuck. I don't think the X pill that I popped helped matters either. Shit I can still go a few more rounds, but I think you've learned your lesson for tonight. I can tell no other nigga has been in my shit though. So, I apologize for that little misunderstanding.

You know I don't play around with what's mine. I'm going to swing back through after I handle those bitches. Be a little more hospitable next time. Your little evil ass makes me take the pussy now. Just give the shit up. It will make it easier on the both of us. Now come and give me a kiss beautiful." He ordered.

I slowly stood to my feet and limped over to that psychotic, arrogant asshole.

He snatched me into his arms and roughly planted his moist lips on mine.

"I want to kiss her too," he stated kneeling down in front of me.

Using his index and middle finger to part my labia, he expertly plunged his thick tongue into my dripping hole. Lapping up all his cum, he replied with a huge smile, "Damn we taste delicious baby!"

"Oh yeah, I love your hair like that baby."

With that, he was gone as swiftly as he'd come. Locking my bedroom door, I quickly retrieved my sleeping son from his bassinet and held him against my heaving chest as I cried inconsolably. What was I going to do?!

« Chapter 10 Cry Me A River »

The Past "Gladys"

IT HAD BEEN SEVEN MONTHS without Lukas and just as long that I'd been seeing Omar. My dad had been gone for over a year now. Although not a day passed without him crossing my mind dozens of times, I was finally able to make it through the day without breaking down. Despite having Omar and Paige, neither of them were ever able to fill my void.

Omar's schedule was extremely hectic. We cherished each and every stolen moment that we were able to spend together. Medical school was certainly not for the weak. My baby was a soldier. When he wasn't in class, he was at work or studying. His discipline was impressive. Most of our peers were partying their college days away, but not Omar and I.

After a long discussion with Paige, she became a little more discreet with her late-night rendezvous. She started either meeting the guys in their dorm rooms, hotels or busting it open in their cars. I had grown sick of walking in on her pale tail tooting it up for every Dom, Rick and Larry, willing to pay. I had to admit, homegirl was making some serious money.

She was able to pay her tuition, bills and still look like she'd stepped off the cover of a fashion magazine. I still preferred that she find a regular job, but I knew that they'd never offer her enough to keep up with her lifestyle. All I could do was continue to pray for her safety every day.

Lying in bed one night, I heard someone begin to knock

loudly on my door. Pulling my comforter over my head, I snuggled deeper into my bed. Whoever it was, would have to come back another time. Drifting back off to sleep, I jumped as the loud knocking grew in both intensity and frequency. Finally glancing over at my nightstand, my clock read 3:42 AM.

I couldn't help but to think, '*Who on Earth would be knocking on my door at this hour?*' I glanced over at Paige's side of the room and noticed that she wasn't there.

Suddenly, an overwhelming fear gripped me as I groggily slid out of bed. As my feet met with the cold floor, I couldn't help but think that perhaps something bad had happened to Paige. Why else would someone be knocking on my door like the police at this hour???

Finally reaching the door, I yelled, "Who is it?!"

We didn't have a peephole so whoever it was would either identify themselves or remain standing on the other side of the door.

"Baby it's me. Open up!" Omar replied.

Quickly snatching the scarf off my head and smoothing my hair down with my hands, I opened the door.

"Omar, baby, is everything okay?" I asked, my voice full of concern.

"No, it isn't Gladys. Can I come in? Is P here?" He inquired looking over at her side of the room.

Stepping back and allowing him entrance into my room I answered, "No, apparently, she's pulling an all-nighter again. I haven't seen her all day. Can I get you something to drink?"

Shaking his head, he replied, "No thanks babe. I'm okay. I actually came over here because I needed to talk to you about something important."

Walking over to my bed, I sat down and turned on my lamp. Glancing at Omar I shrieked, "Oh my goodness baby! What happened to your face?!"

His face, shirt and hands were covered in blood, scrapes and edema. His mouth was busted open. Someone had done a number on him. Jumping up before he could reply, I retrieved some ice, zip lock bags and my first aid kit. I never thought that I'd ever actually have to use it.

As I worked on cleansing, bandaging and icing Omar up, he relayed the events that led him to my house. He stated that he was trying to study for an important exam scheduled for the next day but his roommates were intent on throwing a party. Omar stated that he'd allowed it under the premise that the party would be over by 2:00 AM.

When two came and went with no signs of the party ending, Omar confronted his inebriated roommates. The argument became heated and before he knew what was going on, the three of them commenced to violently attacking him. He reported that somehow, he was able to escape and make it to his car.

He no longer felt safe there and refused to return even for his belongings. As he recounted his ordeal, the both of us cried together as we prayed for God to soften the hearts of his ex-roommates. He came over tonight to see if it were okay if he moved into my family home. Of course, I told him that he could as long as he kept it clean. Since the house was paid off, I refused to charge him rent. He was however responsible for his own utilities.

I was blessed and honestly just wanted to be a blessing to

others. Although he had begged me to move back into my home to be with him, I refused. While I had broken my promise to both God and my daddy already, I refused to shack up with a man who wasn't my husband. Nonetheless Omar was greatly appreciative and commenced to thanking my body over and over again until we both had to get up and rush off to our respective classes.

The sex hadn't improved much at all. I often had to run off and finish the job myself. I'd scream and moan in order to make him think that he was sending me off into orgasmic oblivion...however me and Ms. Kitty knew better. I really liked him and didn't want to hurt his feelings, by telling him that his sex was less than stellar. Aside from leaving me sexually frustrated, he was a great guy. I told myself that it was God's way of punishing me for having premarital sex.

While I had nothing to compare it to, I knew deep down that it had to be better than what he was dishing out. He was clueless in the foreplay department. There was absolutely no romance. I was so disappointed that I'd broken my promise to abstain from sex only to leave each encounter hornier than when we started. I knew eventually the sensitive conversation had to take place...I just prayed that he'd get better before that happened.

Those were the times when I'd fantasize about Lukas the most. Somehow, I knew that sex with him was amazing. The way that he walked, talked and carried himself spoke volumes. His stance alone told me that he possessed a third leg. I had to keep him off my mind!

∞

Being a winter baby, you'd think that I loved the cold weather, snow and winter holidays. I loathed the cold weather and hated driving in the snow even more. I now dreaded my birthday which happened to fall on Christmas because that was the day my father died. I would never feel celebratory on that day ever again. It was now tainted. My once happiest day was now one of dread.

To make my winter blues even worst, I had been stuck in the bed with the flu for the past week. I had never had the flu before, but the symptoms were comparable to death itself. Every muscle in my body ached. My body was running fevers high enough to fry eggs on. I was having simultaneous vomiting and diarrhea episodes. It was not a pretty sight. Embarrassingly enough, I wasn't able to make it to the toilet every time.

I was grateful to have my very own med student caring for me. He catered to my every need as much as his schedule allowed. I was staying at my family home until I recovered. Omar made me soup and ensured that I was replacing the electrolytes that I'd been losing. He assisted me with my showers and made sure to pick up all my homework for me. Omar was even kind enough to take care of my bills for me. I had granted him access to one of my accounts in case of an emergency.

I couldn't have made it without him since Paige was out of town. She'd gone to Dallas for a couple of weeks. Omar was a true Godsend, however, I felt like a burden. He was so responsible and would make the perfect husband one day. Through it all, he never forgot to tell me how beautiful I was. However, I knew I looked a hot mess!

Despite Omar's compassion and diligent care, I was still vomiting profusely as the third week approached. Unable to take it anymore, I had him take me to the emergency room. Something had to give! I was so weak that he had to wheel me through the lobby in a wheelchair. My mouth was too dry to answer a lot of the questions the nurse asked, so I allowed Omar to take over.

I sat back and weakly smiled as I watched him comfortably update the staff on my condition in their medical jargon. He was so freaking smart. Everyone was beyond friendly there. They collected urine, drew labs and thoroughly assessed me from head to toe. They were concerned because they could tell how dehydrated I was by my mucous membranes as well as by the difficulty they faced while attempting to insert an IV.

After four attempts, they were able to successfully insert and IV in my left hand. They proceeded to administer a bolus of a liter of normal saline. I believe I heard one of the nurses' mention replacing some electrolytes as well, but I'm not exactly sure.

At some point I must have dozed off, because I was being awakened by the emergency room doctor. He introduced himself as Dr. Patel. He told me that I was severely dehydrated and that he wanted to admit me overnight for observation. He told me that I definitely had the flu.

His next question puzzled me.

"Gladys, when was your last menstrual period?" He asked.

I thought long and hard, but drew a blank.

"I don't remember." I stated honestly.

"Well, according to your tests, you are pregnant. Congratulations!" He chirped beaming at both Omar and I before heading out of the door.

I was too sick and too stunned to verbally respond. Thoughts of how screwed I was took over my mind. I watched in dismay as Omar grab his coat and heatedly storm out of my hospital room. I probably would have burst out in tears, had I not been too dehydrated to produce some.

« Chapter 11 Mama's Baby, Mr. Monroe's Maybe »

The Past "Celeste"

WITH MY EYES STILL CLOSED, I listened as a familiar voice poured his heart out. Unaware that I was awake, Eli softly stroked my forehead as he professed his love for me. He apologized over and over for cheating on me. He again reported not knowing that Kennedy was my sister. He vowed to make it up to me. His next confession had me ready to lodge a bullet between his eyes.

I involuntarily grimaced as he said, "Cee Cee, I am so sorry for having your car towed. I just wanted you to have to come and talk to me. I ran out of options and knew that you'd reach out to me to discuss the car. It's just that, you refused to allow me anywhere near you. I admit, it was a bitch move, but I promise it was all out of love.

I was desperate and was missing you like crazy. I've already returned your car baby. Again, I am so sorry. I promise that I will always take care of you...no matter what. I'll always have your back even if you decide that you never want to come back to me. You deserve the world and I want to see to it that you get it."

As soon as he finished talking, the door to my room opened. I then heard an equally familiar, yet menacing voice say, "Who the fuck are you?! Little nigga, if you don't get your ass up out of my daughter's room...we are going to have some serious problems!"

There was a brief moment of silence before I heard what I assumed were Eli's footsteps leaving the hospital room. I held my breath as I heard the door close.

I then heard Mr. Monroe say, "Gladys, did you see that shit? I bet her fast ass is fucking him. I should probably put her ass on the stroll, at least she'd be profiting from fucking around with these little young niggas. Oh and make sure her ass doesn't talk to these nosy ass muthafuckas in here when she wakes up. I have enough heat on my ass without having to explain why I pushed her stupid ass down the stairs."

"Lukas, honey, things went way too far this time. Did you have to push her?" My mom finally spoke up for once.

A loud slap could be heard, followed by a startled yelp from my mother.

"Bitch don't you ever question me! I told you it was an accident. I didn't mean to push her, something just came over me. I felt disrespected by her coming in at all hours of the night. I will not tolerate disrespect from you or her in my house." He scolded.

"I cannot do this anymore Lukas. I refuse to continue to sit back and allow you to treat my daughter like this. I've already started the process of filing for a divorce. You can keep it all. I don't want a thing from you. I just want out of this mistake that we call a marriage. This is the straw that has broken the camel's back.

I've loved you wholeheartedly for twenty years and put up with so much abuse and neglect because I didn't know any better. I tolerated so much from you hoping that things would get better between us, but they never did. Your drinking has changed you for the worst. It will take a lifetime to make it up to her.

A mother's job is to protect her children and I have failed miserably. Both times! I don't know how, but I will spend the rest of my life making it up to her. You told me that you'd always love and treat her as your own...but I bet you've never tossed your precious Kennedy down a staircase." She announced in a shaky voice.

I could not believe what I was hearing! What did she mean 'both times'?! 'Treat me like his own?' My life felt like one horrible soap opera. First, I found out that my life long nemesis was in fact my sister. Then it was brought to my attention in front of the entire school that my then boyfriend, Eli was fucking this sister. To make matters worse, Eli initially only pursued me based on a bet to pop my cherry.

Eli had just confessed that he was behind my car's disappearance. Consequently by him having my car towed, it led to me coming home hours after my parents were expecting me. As a result, Mr. Monroe just admitted that he had pushed me down the stairs. Perhaps the most shocking thing out of my parents' entire exchange was the fact that my dad...was not my dad.

To be perfectly honest, my feelings about this were conflicted. On one hand, that explained why he was so resentful towards me. It also explained how he could abuse me the way he had and not give two shits about it. I now knew why he'd always insisted that I call him Mr. Monroe instead of dad. On the other hand, I had so many questions. I felt betrayed.

Who was my real father? Where was he? Did I look like him? Did he know about me? Did he love me? How'd my mother and Mr. Monroe get together. Since Mr. Monroe was not my biological father, that also meant that Kennedy was not really my sister either. Did I have any siblings out there somewhere? Who was I? I felt as if my entire life...my existence was based on lies.

Hell, was my real name even Celeste?!

"G, look baby, no need to go making idle threats. You and *OUR* daughter aren't going anywhere. I may not always show it, but I love the hell out of both of you. Now whatever arrangements you've made to divorce me, stops today. I'm going to go to rehab and I'm even prepared to go to marriage counseling and attend anger management classes, if you think it will help us. I don't want to lose you baby." He vowed, sounding sincere.

Thinking back, I couldn't exactly remember being pushed down the stairs. I vaguely remembered hearing a voice, but thought I'd imagined it. I assumed that I'd tripped and fell based on listening to the doctors and nurses report off to one another at my bedside. I guess that was just the story my mother had fed to them. I couldn't believe he was evil enough to do this to me.

I was banged up pretty badly. According to the hospital staff, I sustained two broken fingers, cervical sprain, a broken femur and four fractured ribs. I had been awake for two days, but had yet to make it known to others. I don't know why, I just wasn't ready to face my issues. The nurses made sure that I received continuous pain medications around the clock and I loved the feeling of numbness. I was pain free for once.

I had a huge cast on my left leg and a c-collar stabilizing my neck and spine. I could feel that my two fractured fingers were buddy wrapped as well. I was in for a long recovery. I'd need physical and occupational therapy once I was discharged from the hospital. One of the benefits of being at Mercy Hospital was the fact that I had a private room.

Guttural moans and the rough slapping of skin pulled me away from my thoughts. Risking detection, I slowly opened my left eye so that I could quickly inspect my surroundings. Much to my disgust, Mr. Monroe had my mother pinned to the wall with her dress hiked up above her waist. With her back to him and his to me, I noted that his pants were down around his knees.

I got a front row seat of his large balls swinging back and forth as he plowed into my stupid mother. Having had enough of watching his ass muscles flex, I snapped my left eye shut again. As the smell of their sex permeated the air, I prayed that they'd hurry the hell up and leave my room. The level of their disrespect nagged at my soul.

Who fucks in front of their hospitalized daughter?! Unconscious or not...it just wasn't right. Hearing his pace quicken, I was all too pleased as I heard their sweaty flesh connect for the final time before he shot off his highly anticipated load.

Quickly reassembling themselves, my mother walked over to me and kissed me on the forehead. They stayed for what I estimated to be about fifteen minutes before they left. After hearing the door close, I swiftly opened my eyes. Reaching for the room freshener that my nurse had left on my bedside to mask my incontinent episodes, I generously sprayed my room.

Satisfied that I'd successfully annihilated their musky scent, I laid back onto my pillow spent. Just completing that one task winded me. Deciding that I would continue to pretend to be unconscious for two more days, I drifted back off to La La Land.

« Chapter 12 Show Me State »

The Past "Mike"

"MIKE! MIKE! WHAT THE hell are you doing you black son of a bitch?! Let me go!!!"

Chuckling, I shook my head in amusement. Only this bitch would continue to talk shit at a time like this.

"Look baby, I'm sorry...in fact *we* are sorry for what we did to your little baby mama." Tamar stated motioning between herself and her friend Shay.

I continued to ignore her ass just as I had been for the past three days. She had admitted that she'd told Alicia that she wasn't into torture prior to coldly shooting her. Unfortunately for her, I was. I was intent on making both of those bitches suffer for what they did to my girl and son. True, I still had love for Tamar, but what she did was unforgivable.

Her pleas and promises to disappear and never return fell on deaf ears. They both had to die in order for me to get my family back. Alicia and I would raise both Sincere and Michaela together.

Three days ago, I had called Tamar apologizing and begging to come back home. I told her how much I missed her and our daughter. I then begged to come over. Once I got to Tamar's house, we talked for a while before I decided that I wanted some pussy. I told her that we were going to drop Michaela off at my house so that my mother could baby sit for us.

After dropping my princess off, I lied and told Tamar that I needed to make a quick stop at the warehouse where I stored some of my stolen merchandise. I also sold her on the idea of being able to grab a few items for herself. That bitch was always down for any cause that enabled her to walk away with something free.

Once arriving at the warehouse, I killed the engine. It was hot and muggy outside. I was thankful that I had the utilities cut on in the warehouse. Otherwise it would have been intolerable in there. Once going into the building, I played it cool. I was my usual charming self. Looking over at Tamar, I hated the bitch with a passion for what she'd done to my family.

I blamed her for the entire demise of me and Alicia's relationship. Had it not been for her money grubbing, baby trapping ass, we would still be on good terms. However, her red leggings coupled with my desire to kill her ass had my dick standing at attention. I had to admit, I had some bad ass baby mamas. Too bad this bitch's days were numbered.

Tamar had accompanied me to the warehouse several times before. However, I never allowed Alicia to be exposed to this type of shit. After unlocking the door and deactivating the security system, she wasted no time darting off to where the stolen clothing was stored. Watching her thumb through some of the most expensive shit that I had, I couldn't help but to shake my head. She was so predictable.

Focusing back on my erection, I had decided that I was going to fuck her one last time. I figured I'd fuck her now, because beyond today, she'd be pissing and shitting on herself as I implemented my torturous plans. Today would most likely be the last day that I'd view her as fuckable.

Walking up behind her, I wrapped my body around hers

while taking in her fresh scent. She always smelled so edible. She wasn't much of a housekeeper or a cook, but she kept her body spic and span. Grinding my pelvis into her succulent ass, my hands explored the anterior aspect of her body. Tilting her head to the side, I suckled on the nape of her neck as she drew in a haggard breath.

Each of my hands claimed a nipple as our bodies swayed to imaginary music. Feeling her warm breast milk seep onto my hands, had me spinning her around. She had exceeded her breast pumping window. Her swollen titties were engorged with milk. Being the amazingly observant man that I was, I knew how uncomfortable Tamar got when this happened.

Gently lifting her up onto a table, I grabbed her right tit and began to suckle like a starved baby. While sucking on Tamar's titty, she assisted me in taking off her tights by lifting her ass up off the table. I ripped her panties off and pocketed them so that I could smell them in the future...should I miss her after she was gone.

Pulling my dick out of the zipper hole, I slowly sank into her wetness. Switching to her left titty, I proceeded to deliver slow, deep strokes to her pussy as I continued to drain her milk. This must have really turned her on because I was sloshing all inside of her. She had the front of my jeans soaked.

Feeling the urge to cum prematurely, I pulled out and said, "Suck my dick."

Being the freak that she was, Tamar quickly obliged. She didn't let minor glitches such as sucking her own pussy juices off my dick stop her. In fact, before I could blink, she had my entire pipe down her esophagus, yet she was still trying to find room for my nuts. This is a prime example of why I cheated on Alicia. To keep it real, I couldn't even get her prudish ass to suck my dick. Damn I was going to miss Tamar!

My head fell backwards as I relished the feeling that Tamar was giving me. With my arms resting behind my head, I thrusted my hips forward as I committed to fucking her pretty face. Her mouth was so warm and wet, while her lips were pillow soft.

After about ten minutes, I pulled her up by her hair and bent her over the table. Smearing her thick love juice over my dick and onto her asshole, I slowly pushed her anal walls aside to accommodate my girth. Her tightness gripped me so snuggly, that I almost lost it as soon as I entered her body. I was never able to last long when I was in the back door.

I pounded away at her asshole fast and furious despite her pained cries. I loved creating those loud farting sounds as air escaped her asshole. It always embarrassed the fuck out of her and her body would tense up. I always had to reassure her that I loved hearing that shit.

As I felt my nut rising for a second time, I figured now would be an appropriate time to render her defenseless. As I continued tapping that ass mercilessly, I wrapped my large hands around her delicate neck. I squeezed tightly, but just enough to put her to sleep. I didn't want to kill the bitch...not just yet anyway. I needed her to answer some questions first.

She struggled a little, however my massive frame pressed up against her petite one rendered her efforts useless. I was more than twice her size. Once I heard her snoring, I continued pounding away in order to achieve my nut. As I approached the point of no return, I noticed a sudden foul odor. Ignoring it, I unloaded deep inside of Tamar's ass.

As I pulled out, I noticed that her unconscious ass had painted my wood with a fresh coat of steaming hot excrement.

Once completely removed from her body, several brown turds plopped onto the ground near my brand-new sneakers.

"You nasty ass muthafucka!" I scolded an unconscious Tamar.

As disgusted and pissed as I was, I knew she had no control over her bowels at the moment. The bitch was lucky that shit didn't land on my shoes. I'd give her a pass for now. Wiping my dick off on her white shirt, I then drug her shitty ass over to a chair that I had assigned to her. After tying and securing her with tape, I quickly darted off to the nearest bathroom.

I grabbed some soapy paper towels and commenced to scrubbing the black off my dick in the bathroom. I couldn't wait to take an actual shower. Regrettably for me, the shower would have to wait. I needed to stick around until her poop butt ass woke up so that she could give me the whereabouts on her friend, Shay.

∞

After about an hour, I saw Tamar starting to rouse in the chair. I had already dimmed the lights for the shock factor. I wanted her to wake up and initially not know what the fuck happened or how she got here. She couldn't see me at first, but I saw every detail of her worried face. I could tell that she was terrified.

Once she took in her surroundings and realized that she was secured to the chair, she spazzed. She began to scream for me...so I assumed it was all slowly coming back to her. Walking within her central vision, she proceeded to curse me the fuck out. She called me every name in the book. I let her vent before walking up to her and slapping fire to her disrespectful ass. For a second, I thought I'd broken her neck with the way it snapped back.

She immediately began crying.

Her tears tugged at my heart strings a little because my daughter made the same faces when she cried.

"Why Mike? Why are you doing this to me? To us? All I ever tried to do was love you bae." She cried.

"T, I'm sure if you think deep and hard, you will know exactly why we are here. However, I am the one who needs some questions answered." I replied.

"You want to know where to find Shay? Well I'm not telling your punk ass shit! I ain't no snitching ass bitch. If you want her, you are going to have to play Inspector Gadget and find her yourself. You know you're not gonna do shit to us. Untie me so that I can go and get my damn baby, boy!" She angrily spat.

I laughed at her bipolar ass. One minute she was professing her love for me and now she was snapping at me.

"Bitch, I see that you think this shit here is a game. You two jealous ass bitches almost killed not only my girl, but also my son. My *son*, T! You caused him to be delivered a month early. You were also behind him being hooked up to a bunch of tubes and machines. How would you have felt if our baby girl had to go through that shit?! Because of you, he spent the first month of his life in the hospital. His mother was forced to undergo a potentially unnecessary C-section.

You know, I sneak in and just watch Alicia sleep sometimes. She's always extra beautiful when she's asleep. Besides, lately it's the only time I can seem to get near her. Because of your brutal attack, she wakes up screaming most nights. You had my girl scared to come outside and shit.

So, you see, this is most certainly not a game Tamar. Now, I am going to ask you once. Where can I find Shay? Every time you lie or ignore the question, it will result in you losing a finger. Once we run out of fingers, we will move down to your toes. The choice is yours baby mama. Hell, I'm free all-night long." I seriously stated.

"Like I told your bitch ass before, I'm not telling you shit nigga! Do what you feel is necessary!" She countered.

This hoe thought I was bluffing. Turning on my heels to retrieve my various torture devices, I thought to myself how I was going to have to show her ass. After all, this was the **Show Me** state! I was all too happy to oblige her. It had been a while since I'd had to use my kit.

Grabbing a hold of her hand, I had decided against using my self-made finger slicer. My finger slicer could completely sever a finger in less than a tenth of a second. It was nearly painless...at first anyway. The beauty of it was that it always left a squeaky-clean cut. This was important if reattachment were being considered. Since she was being a bitch, I was going back and forth between a machete and a good old-fashioned kitchen knife. Right about now, I wanted to use a box cutter.

Being the nice guy that I am, I decided to use the machete. It was nowhere near as good as my finger slicer, however, it was an upgrade from the kitchen knife. If she continued acting the way she had been, then she would find herself quickly downgraded to the kitchen knife.

Firmly grabbing her left pinky finger, I swiftly removed it with the machete. She screamed a loud, pained cry. Blood instantly spurted from her now detached nub. Not wanting her to bleed out today, I quickly grabbed a lighter and burned off her bleeding vessels. The smell of her burning flesh sent a wave of nausea through me. Her tortured cries echoed through the large warehouse. I then wrapped her tender nub with gauze.

Giving her a few minutes to recuperate, I decided to spark up a blunt. I prayed that by smoking, it would give me the patience I needed to complete my job.

"Baby mama, are you ready to talk now? Where is Shay?" I prodded.

"Fuck you Mike! I told you I ain't telling you shit!" She hissed with saliva spewing from her angry mouth.

"Damn, so it's like that T? Does that no edge having hoe mean that much to you? Suit yourself, you stupid bitch!" I spat growing impatient.

I placed my lit blunt up to her neck and watched her skin sizzle. I repeated this process several times until the blunt was put completely out. The screams from Tamar, pierced my ear drums.

"Ahhhhhh!!! Mike stop! I fucking hate you!!!" She bellowed in agony.

Grabbing the machete again, I swiftly chopped off both her left index and middle fingers. She had pissed me the fuck off so the bitch owed me two fingers this time. I was tired of playing Mr. Nice Guy with her ass. She cried inconsolably as she looked at her mangled hand. All that remained on her left hand was her thumb and ring finger. Dark blood dripped onto the floor as she appeared to be becoming delirious. I suppose the pain was just too much.

Just as I was about to dress those wounds and call it quits for the night, I heard Tamar faintly whisper, "Grand."

"What was that T?" I inquired.

"Sh...Shay. She lives on 1116 Grand Blvd. It's a small blue house on the corner." She whispered, barely audible.

With that, I thanked her by two piecing her ass. She instantly went unconscious. I was hoping that she'd sleep until I returned.

After securing the warehouse, I jumped into my car with murder on my mind. I had met Shay a few times and never had any issues with her in the past. She seemed decent enough, but she had to pay for what went down with Alicia. After all, you are the company you keep.

Riding past Popeyes, my stomach loudly rumbled. I decided to pull over and grab some chicken to go. I didn't know how long I'd get stuck casing out this bitch's house, but I wanted to start the night off with a full stomach. Roughly snatching my bag from the rude ass bitch in the drive-thru window, I quickly sped off.

Pulling up to the address that Tamar had given me, I killed the engine. All the lights appeared to be out inside of the house. I wondered how many people lived in that muthafucka. When Tamar mentioned that the house was small, she had exaggerated. That blue bitch was nearly nonexistent. The wooden porch was rundown and I noticed clothes hanging in the windows.

"Ghetto muthafuckas." I said to myself.

Prepping myself for a long night, I reclined my seat and removed my box of chicken from the bag. Upon opening my box, I instantly saw red. These chicken frying bitches *always* got my order wrong. No matter how big or small. The crazy thing is, I'd repeated the order numerous times. That chicken bitch was next on my hit list. She'd be seeing me very soon.

Popeyes always made me feel close to Alicia. That girl could eat there every day of the week and never grow tired of it.

∞

Three hours after pulling up to the little blue house, I was awakened by the closing of a car door. I was slipping! I guess that *ITIS* had gotten the best of me.

After wiping sleep out of my heavy eyes, I focused on the figure in front of me. I became annoyed upon realizing that Shay was not alone. However, I was not going to allow another nigga's presence to deter me from completing my mission. Unfortunately for him, he was simply with the wrong bitch at the wrong time. Again, you are the company you keep.

Instead of grabbing my heat, I opted to use my favorite serrated knife. My .380 didn't have a silencer and I didn't want to draw any unnecessary attention to us. Before exiting my car, I also grabbed my chloroform soaked rag.

I slowly crept up behind the two giggling love birds. I couldn't believe that I was able to get so close to them without being detected. They had to be under the influence of something. I figured that I'd take care of the nigga first since he posed the biggest physical threat...or so I thought.

Just before they reached the steps that led to the tiny house, I grabbed his chunky ass and swiftly sliced his jugular vein with lighting speed.

He died without ever seeing me coming. Blood sprayed all over me and Shay...she just didn't realize it yet. Roughly dropping that nigga on the hard steps, I wiped his fresh blood from my face. Maybe, I should have just snapped his neck or something. It would've been much cleaner. Oh well, it was too late to cry over spilled blood now.

"Hey Domm, can you unlock the door?" Shay asked still oblivious to the fact that Domm's ass had expired.

"Sure baby, let me get that for you." I snidely replied, anticipating her reaction.

"What the fu...!" She started to scream as I rushed her.

She surprised me with her speed. She somehow dodged me as I attempted to tackle her ass on the raggedy porch. She screamed loudly as she finally noticed Domm lifelessly lying on the first step. His blood was everywhere. After brushing past me, she soared down the six steps and fled towards her car.

The bitch must have forgotten how athletic I was too. I swiftly caught up to her as she reached the rear of her car. She was still screaming, which infuriated me. Wrapping my hands around her neck, I squeezed tightly until she agreed to shut the fuck up.

After she agreed to behave, I doused the rag with more of the chloroform and walked her over to my trunk. Seeing my trunk open must have freaked her out because she proceeded to punch me in my face before once again turning to run. My blood sprayed all over my shirt and new shoes. I was livid. I quickly snatched her back by her ponytail. She turned around and clawed my neck and chest with her nails.

The crazy bitch then kneed me in my nuts which immediately brought me to my knees. Luckily, I never loosened the death grip that I had on her ponytail. Quickly composing myself, I throat punched her rambunctious ass. She was definitely a fighter. As I watched her drop to the floor grasping her neck, I knew that we had to move fast.

I heard sirens in the distance and knew it was only a matter of time before 5-0 caught up to us. One of her nosy ass neighbors called the law on me. I wished I knew which one because I'd definitely come back and pay them a visit. Taking the soaked rag that I had prepared for her, I place it over her nose and mouth as I observed her inhaling deeply. She was still winded and struggling for air since I had punched her in the throat.

Once she was asleep, I picked up her athletic body and crudely tossed her into my trunk. Quickly surveying the premises to ensure I hadn't left any evidence behind, I jumped into my car and sped away just as blue and red lights circled around the corner.

« Chapter 13 Playing Hooky »

The Past "Eli"

"**MAN GET OUT OF MY** face with that bullshit! Ain't nobody trying to listen to that fabricated shit girl! What yo stanking ass needs to do is find out who yo real baby daddy is, because that nigga is not me!" I fumed glaring at Gia's stupid ass.

I was headed to school when she had called me up asking me to stop by and knock her back out. Honestly, I wasn't all that interested since Kennedy's mama couldn't join us. That bitch was being very distant lately. She must have finally decided to become a parent instead of the hoe that I had always known her to be.

True to her word, Ken hadn't reached out to me since the picnic fiasco. Although all that shit needed to come out, the timing and the place were off. Kennedy could have gone about the entire ordeal a better way. Celeste was still in the hospital. I hated seeing her connected to all that shit. I'd trade places with her any day. She didn't deserve that shit...I did.

I can't believe that I'd fucked up the best thing that had ever happened to me. They say that you never know what you have until you lose it and trust me, truer words have never been spoken. Celeste was something that I wasn't even aware that I wanted until I had lost her. My family even loved the fuck out of Cee Cee. I prayed like never before that she would pull through this.

I visited her every day, careful to avoid her parents. I also didn't want her bitch ass pops to recognize and remember who the fuck I was. I'm a firm believer in the element of surprise. I had her car placed back in front of her house, but not before having it fully detailed.

Now as I sat on Gia's living room couch, I was a raging bull. This hoe had killed my high. I should have known the bitch was up to no good as soon as I came into the door. Normally there isn't much conversing between the two of us. If it isn't about fucking then what else is there to discuss?

When I came in, she had slow music playing in the background. She had strawberries, grapes, wine and cheese tantalizingly displayed on the coffee table in front of us. It was cute and all but a nigga was fucking starving! I would have been more impressed by a T-bone steak, potatoes, corn and some ice cold red Kool-Aid.

The flavor was insignificant.

I was initially in a good mood so I decided to keep my disappointment to myself. She proceeded to give me a long sensual massage as she fed me the fruit and cheese. It was a very nice gesture and all, but I was ready to hit so that I could go and get some grown man food. Just as I was about to order her to sit on my dick, Gia gave me a serious look and told me that we needed to talk.

Those are four words that you never want a jump off to say to you. It could only mean one of two things...possibly even both. Either she was burning or she was knocked up. I truly wasn't prepared to hear either option. Instead of speaking, I motioned for her to get whatever she needed to say out by motioning with my hands. She looked beyond uncomfortable...scared even.

This was surprising because she was nobody's punk. Not by a long shot. Her behavior made me even more nervous as I anticipated the worse possible scenario.

"Eli, I'm just going to give it to you straight. I'm pregnant. I don't know exactly how far along I am, but I suspect it happened that day we went at it raw. Before you even fix your mouth to ask me, yes, it is your baby. Despite what you may think about me, I'm not a hoe. I've been chillin when I'm not with you. I just thought that I should let you know.

I do not believe in abortions. I won't force you to help out, but I'd like for you to since I didn't create this life alone. I'm not an idiot and my expectations are realistic. I know you will never be with me no more than you were with Ken, but I hope that we can co-parent."

To be perfectly honest with you, I didn't hear shit she said after she announced that she was pregnant. The shit sounded like blah, blah, blah, blah, blah! I felt like I was looking through someone else's eyes and listening with someone else's ears because this just could not be my life right now.

I couldn't picture being tied down to her ass for life in any capacity. She may be preaching that 'I'll raise my baby alone' shit now, but once she got a taste of how expensive babies are she wouldn't hesitate to put me on papers. She could miss me with that load of bullshit. I was practically raising my little brother and sister, so I knew firsthand how financially draining kids could be. I also knew this broke, unemployed muthafucka wasn't raising no baby solo.

"Gia, I don't know why you are telling me all that shit, but you and I both know that isn't my baby. I only hit once without a condom and I pulled out before I came. What type of sucka do you take me for? Nice try though. I suggest you find your real kid's father. But on that note, I'm out!" I replied.

I was pissed! First, she blew my high and now I was leaving with a heavy nut sack. "Dumb bitch!" I said to her while walking past her tearful ass.

After making it to my car, I remembered that my grandmother had cooked a large Sunday dinner the day before. I knew we had plenty of mouthwatering leftovers. Instead of wasting money on some mediocre fast food, I hightailed it home in record time.

Opening up the fridge, I did my infamous, 'I'm about to fuck this food up dance.' I was definitely one of those niggas who sang and danced while eating a great meal. I didn't sing or dance once at Gia's with that damn fruit she fed me. Wack ass bitch!

My eyes grew as big as saucers as I opened up the first container and saw my granny's fried chicken. Grabbing two of the biggest pieces, I then grabbed the pans containing mac and cheese, sweet potatoes, cabbage, fried corn and corn bread. I placed my plate in the microwave and proceeded to pour myself a glass of lemonade.

Once the microwave beeped indicating that my food was ready to be consumed, I hurriedly rushed over to retrieve it. Just as I was about to open the door to the microwave, I heard a loud thump from above. I instantly became alarmed and grabbed my .380 from its clip.

No one should have been home. My brother and sister were at school and my grandmother typically hung out with her sister on Mondays. They had their little hair appointment rituals every week. Someone apparently knew our schedules and were trying to rob us. Why hadn't the alarm gone off? How'd they get in?

Glancing around cautiously, I didn't see anything missing or out of place. I decided to creep upstairs. Whoever was in here was about to meet their maker. This was the ultimate violation and was punishable by death. What would they have done to my granny if she had still been in the house?

I moved slowly, careful not to make the floor creak beneath my weight. My adrenaline level was off the charts. I couldn't wait to empty my clip into whoever was upstairs. Finally reaching the landing, I carefully peeked into my granny's room. Nothing was out of the ordinary in there. I then passed my little brother's bedroom and the upstairs bathroom and noticed nothing unusual in those areas either. Finally reaching the last room on the left side of the hallway, I took a deep breath as I roughly flung the door open.

I had my gun drawn and my right index finger on the trigger as I took in the most disappointing vision of my life. My little fourteen-year-old sister, Malia, was on top of some nigga riding the shit out of him. I was frozen in place. Was I really bearing witness to my little sister having sex?! Not only having sex, but experienced sex. This was certainly not her first rodeo.

I was beyond hurt. It was in that moment that I felt remorseful for having sex with other people's sisters' that I had in the past. The visual was painful. By this time, Malia had jumped off the nigga and called herself hiding under the covers. It was in that moment that I noticed Trey's nasty ass lying next to my sister. This overgrown nigga was at least twenty and had a kid already.

The crazy thing is his baby momma, Pinky was a good woman. Trey was that same fuck nigga who made Cee Cee grab his little dick last year on her birthday. I remember owing him an ass whooping for the way he stared at her back then too. He was way too old to be fucking with my little sister. What had possessed her to be so stupid!

My disappointment, hurt and sadness was instantly replaced with rage, homicide and hatred. I was seeing pure red as I rushed that muthafucka. I pushed Malia's naked ass out of the bed and told her to get the fuck out of the room. My first two punches connected with Trey's jaw. I instantly heard his jaw break.

I then preceded to pistol whoop his perverted ass. His weak ass apologies and begging for me to stop fell on deaf ears. I wanted to kill him and I knew that in time I would, however this just wasn't the time or the place.

My sister's screaming snapped me out of my murderous trance. I couldn't barely stand to look at her. I had drilled in her over and over about how these niggas only wanted one thing. She knew the game because she'd learned from the best. Yet she still decided to go out into the streets and hoe around. She knew better however she was acting no different from the rest of the hoes I ran through.

"Malia, I thought I told you to get the fuck out of here! Trey, my nigga, you've just committed suicide by fucking with my sister. You have violated in the worst way. You are twenty fucking with a little ass girl! Nigga you are foul for this shit. Get the fuck up out of my house and you better not ever step foot back inside of this bitch! Don't contact my sister either. And oh, you better sleep with one eye open. You better believe that I'll be coming for your pedophile ass!"

Because he was taking too long to stand on his wobbly legs, I decided to help him along. Grabbing his ass by his braids, I drug that nigga to the top of our stairs before tossing his ass down them. Since he already knew what I was doing, he was able to protect his vital areas.

I slowly descended down after he landed at the bottom. I then continued helping him get the fuck out of my house. Once reaching my porch, I reminded his ass not to come back. Looking to the right, I noticed his raggedy ass car parked down the street. I was so hungry when I had arrived, I hadn't even noticed that piece of shit parked there.

Slamming the door behind me, I yelled for Malia to bring her fast ass downstairs. She was crying so hard snot was running down onto her upper lip. Usually her tears moved me, but not today. I could tell that she was embarrassed because she was avoiding making eye contact with me.

"So, you are out here just fucking these niggas now Lia?" I inquired with hurt in my voice.

"No...no Eli..." She started.

I abruptly cut her off. "So were my eyes deceiving me? Did I not just catch your little ass upstairs fucking that grown ass man under my roof?!" I spat angrily through clenched teeth.

Times like this made me hate having a pretty sister...especially one younger than me.

"Yes, Eli, but he is the only one. I promise. I haven't been with anyone else. He's my boyfriend." She cried.

"That nigga is nothing to you but a distant memory. I better not catch him around this house or you again. Do I make myself clear?! You have me out here looking like a damn fool. How long have you been fucking that nigga?"

"I don't know." She mumbled dismissively.

Her response made me see red again. I walked over to her and slapped fire to her face. Her cheek immediately reddened. I instantly regretted putting my hands on her. I'd never hit my sister before. We both glared at each other in shock for a few moments before she took off sobbing to her room.

Today was a shitty ass day. I should've just taken my ass to school today. I sat down and nibbled on my now lukewarm food. I wasn't even hungry anymore. As soon as I finished, Lia was going to the clinic to be checked out and to receive the morning after pill.

« Chapter 14 In Too Deep »

The Present "Autumn"

A COUPLE OF DAYS HAD passed and the mood in our large house was somber. Mrs. Douglas was still out of town. Sadly, her older sister had suffered another stroke while in the hospital and was unable to recover. Mrs. Douglas had the misfortune of having to make the decision to withdraw life support.

Her older sister, Violet, had never married or had any children. She had also neglected to create a living will. So many people take Father Time for granted. We are always under the misconception that we have so much more time than we actually do. By failing to create a living will, we can be viewed as being selfish. It isn't fair to make our loved ones make such decisions on our behalf.

Mrs. Douglas had opted to cremate her sister. There would be no funeral service. Violet had been a reclusive person in life so Mrs. Douglas decided to mourn her sister's death privately. She felt Violet would have never wanted to be in the spotlight...not even in death.

Don stayed behind to look after the three of us. I still could not believe that he was Wintress's father. His admission literally had me hit the floor. When I went down, I went down hard! When I came to, I was surrounded by the concerned faces of Chris, Landon, MaDonna and Don. That fall left me with a huge goose-egg on the back of my head.

MaDonna took the liberty of making me an ice pack and helping me back to bed. The last thing I should've been doing with a head injury is laying down, but I didn't have the energy or drive for anything else. I had so many questions for Don, however, I couldn't stand to look at his deceitful face at the moment. He disgusted me even more than usual.

MaDonna stayed with me for the rest of that day. We didn't talk much. I slept for the most part...or at least pretended to sleep. I didn't feel like answering any of her bullshit questions. Although I didn't necessarily want to be alone, I really didn't feel like being bothered either.

The next morning, I awoke to birds chirping and my left cheek being stroked. The familiarity of the touch caused my eyes to snap open. I loudly groaned from my pounding headache as well as the stench seeping out of Don's rot mouth. I really hated everything about his existence.

"Autumn, we need to talk." He whispered.

To avoid vomiting from the smell of his foul breath, I turned my back towards him. He took that as a sign that I was just upset with him.

Blowing a frustrated breath, he continued, "I know you're upset with me right now and have a lot of questions that you'd like answered. I'm man enough to admit that I owe it to you to explain everything."

He paused for a second while touching my left shoulder. I guess he was attempting to see if I was paying attention to him.

"When I met your mother, I guess you must have been around four or so. Let me start by saying I loved that woman with everything in me. She was so beautiful and there was an innocence about her that drove me wild. I know it may be strange hearing your mother and innocent in the same sentence...but she was.

I met Celeste through an escort service called ViXXXens that my buddy had recommended. I had always had a thing for black women, but never had the confidence to approach one. Besides in this area, interracial dating wasn't exactly acceptable. It still isn't if you ask me.

When I first met your mother, my jaw literally dropped because of how gorgeous I found her to be. She was so classy and poised. She wasn't dressed scantily as I'd expected her to be. She wore very little makeup and her hair was neatly done in a basic bun. She had the prettiest shy smile and then there were her eyes. Her almond shaped eyes gave her an exotic appearance.

I instantly wondered how a young woman of her caliber would be caught up in the escort business. I wanted to know everything about her. I found her to be so intriguing. She was so well-spoken and was able to converse about any topic brought up.

We went to dinner and just talked for hours during our first "date". We didn't even have sex. Just being in her presence was stimulating enough for me. I wanted to bring her into my world. Unfortunately, she wasn't big on talking about herself. She was a great listener and would give me advice on various topics, but I was not welcomed into her world.

Your mother had become my addiction. I craved her all the time. I spent so much money that eventually she quit ViXXXens altogether. Now she didn't have to share the bulk of her earnings with the company anymore. She took the entire profit home. This made me happy for two reasons. Her schedule for me was now wide open and I no longer had to compete with other guys for her time. Or at least that's what I thought.

The first time that your mother and I made love, it felt like fireworks were being set off between the two of us. It was magical. She was the very first black woman that I'd been with and I haven't looked back since. I've only dated white women publicly to disguise my attraction for black women.

I tried to talk your mother into going to school. Whenever I looked at her, I saw so much untapped potential. She could've achieved anything she set her mind to. I know she loved the hell out of you. Although I'd only met you a few times, her face always lit up whenever she talked about you.

A couple of years into our "relationship" I decided that I no longer wanted to be a paying customer. I wanted to be in a normal relationship with your mother. She all but laughed in my face when I suggested that. She had drastically changed over the years. She went from loving and compassionate to cold and hostile. She went from humble to entitled.

I even proposed to her once, but she said she wasn't ready. I had no clue that she had a drug problem but apparently, she had one long before we'd even met. I think her drug use just worsened with all the money I tricked off with her. It's funny how little you notice when you're enamored with someone. Celeste could do no wrong.

Once I discovered for sure that she was using drugs, I was devastated. By the time I realized what was going on, she was already in too deep. I did everything in my power to get her clean. I blew through so much money sending her to inpatient rehabilitation facilities. I paid for a nanny to be with you during every stint she spent in rehab. I was a damn good man to your mother, but every time she got out, she'd eventually spit in my face by returning to drugs.

As much as it pained me, I had to eventually severe ties with Celeste. I could no longer play the sucker nor the enabler. I still loved her and knew that I'd take her back without a second thought once she got herself together. It was difficult cutting her off completely. We had a few slip ups here and there. She'd come to me with different sob stories that tugged at my heartstrings.

I also made sure that the necessities were taken care of. I never wanted her completely out on the streets. It was during one of those "slip ups" that Wintress was conceived. By this time, your mother was out in the streets bad. Instead of working for an upscale escort company, she was now selling her ass on the streets for a ten-dollar hit."

I turned over glaring at him hatefully for his poor choice of words. Getting the picture, he quickly apologized before continuing.

"Believe me when I say, none of what I am saying is intended to hurt you. You've just been in the dark long enough. It's no secret that your mother was hooking for money and it's no secret that she was a junkie. Those are just cold hard facts.

As I was saying, I didn't even realize that Wintress was mine until a month before she was born. Your mother called me about a month before her due date and informed me that I was the father.

Of course, I was skeptical at first given your mother's track record. She begged me to help her get clean, yet again. She feared that you and Wintress would be taken away if she tested positive for drugs in the hospital.

Against my better judgement, I agreed to help her like always. I don't know why but I could never give up on her. I held out hope that she would eventually grow tired of that lifestyle.

I demanded a DNA test be done immediately after Wintress was born. The truth of the matter is, I would've helped her support the baby regardless. That's how much I loved her. I just needed to know.

I warned your mother that if Wintress was in fact mine, I'd seek full custody. The only issue was, I didn't know how to do that without having to explain to my mother how I met Celeste. How could I explain to my mother that her first and potentially only grandchild was created with a hooking junkie who I was deeply in love with? She wouldn't understand and neither would my mother's uptight inner circle.

I loved my mother too much to bring that type of embarrassment around her. She was still grieving from the loss of my father at that time. She couldn't stomach any more bad news. The results of the DNA test came back and proved that I was 99.997% the father of Wintress. It was a bittersweet moment. I loved having my very own kid with the one and only woman that I'd ever loved.

I just wished that the circumstances were better. I wanted to be a family. If Celeste were able to stay clean, I'd be able to finally introduce you all as my family. I couldn't bring a dope fiend to my mother. In true junkie fashion, Celeste was clean for a little while after she delivered Wintress but soon returned to her old tricks. I always made sure that you and my daughter had what you needed. Every time I threatened to get the both of you taken away, she would move and I would lose touch.

I had tried to have you both placed into our home several times over the years but it was a difficult task. Your mother rarely stayed in the same place for long and would threaten your schools not to divulge if you two were currently enrolled there. Honestly after a while, I grew weary and foolishly gave up.

Forgive me for what I'm about to say, but I grew to despise your mother. She had put me through so much and I realized that she never even loved me. She was an opportunist. All those years and money I had invested in her meant absolutely nothing to her. I was the only person in the world that ever tried to help her, yet she still shit on me every opportunity she got. I felt like a complete idiot.

Life went on. Years went by and I hadn't heard anything from your mother. I prayed for her all the time. I hoped that she had finally gotten her life together for the sake of you and Wintress. Imagine how surprised I was to hear about her tragic murder on the news. That shit brought back all those old feelings from before.

Of course, I didn't learn about your mother's death until the day after it occurred. Wintress was already placed with the Price family. I was only able to get you because your placement was delayed by your hospital stay. Like I told you before, I had to pay a buddy of mine to pull a few strings.

I could have been upfront and confessed to the authorities that I am Wintress's father. I would have been awarded custody immediately since I have a copy of the paternity test. But as I said before, I just didn't want to embarrass my mother. I also didn't want to piss her off and be disinherited. Now I'm pissed because I've lost thirty-five thousand dollars and I still do not have my baby girl with me.

I paid for your mother's funeral. I figured despite how wrong she'd done me, she still deserved a proper burial. She was still so beautiful. Finding out that she was HIV positive scared the living daylights out of me. I always had unprotected sex with her, despite her being heavily in the streets. I knew what she did out there, yet I never viewed her as dirty or anything that I needed to be protected from.

I immediately went to a clinic and was tested. Thankfully that test as well as the two following it have all came back negative. That's what took me so long to make a move on you. I had to make sure that I was negative.

When I look at you, I see all the good times I shared with your mother. You are damn near her exact replica. Sometimes I think you look more like her then she did her damn self. When I saw you and Wintress's pictures on my buddy's desk, I couldn't believe how uncanny the resemblance was between you and your mother. I tried *to resist my urges to be with you, however, it proved to be an impossible feat.*

> *After all, your mother was my addiction. Finding you gave me a second chance to right all my wrongs. I'll never give up on you the way I did Celeste. I love you Celeste and plan on marrying you just as soon as my mother kicks the bucket."*

With tears streaming down my face I replied, "My name is Autumn, I am not Celeste! I am not my fucking mother, Don!"

"Oh, but you are in so many ways. You belong to me and I'm never letting you go." He boasted.

"You're sick! You should get some help. Where is Madonna?" I said in contempt.

"You are really trying my patience Autumn. You truly are. I took MaDonna home. Her grandmother needed her to babysit her siblings. I was ready for her cock blocking ass to go anyway." He replied.

"So, what is the plan? How are we going to find my sister?" I questioned, ignoring his comments about Donna.

"Trust me, I have two of the best private investigators looking for her. We are getting warm, trust me. Those fuckers are going to pay for what they've done. You don't take my money and then kidnap my kid and expect to live to tell about it. Wintress will be home soon, I promise." He whispered into the crook of my neck.

With that he spread my legs apart exposing my bare pussy. I watched in disgust as his fat face lit up like a Christmas tree. He quickly placed his large balding head in between my thighs. I silently wept as he merrily slurped away at my lower lips.

I was filled with worry as thoughts of my little sister's whereabouts clouded my mind. Where the fuck are you Wintress???!!! I externally screamed as I loudly unloaded into that fat bastard's mouth.

« Chapter 15 Goodbye, Berry's Cherry »

The Past "Lukas"

"AYE, WHAT CAN I do for you today Mr. Berry?" I inquired with a devious smirk adorning my handsome face.

"Hey youngster, I ummmm, I need my usual. But listen, I'm a little short today. I had to spend most of the money. I had to keep the lights on. It's been slow at my daughter's job so she needed me to help out with the electric bill this month. I swear I can give you the difference on Thursday. Please man, I'm sick!" He pleaded.

I stared at his pitiful ass for a few moments. He was jonsing bad! His nose was running and he was scratching and shit. He looked like he hadn't showered in days...maybe even weeks. I couldn't have been happier about the monster I'd created. Mr. Berry was now my puppet. my *Lukette* to be exact.

"Nigga, I done told your stupid ass before that I don't do credit. I need money, jewelry, electronics, collateral of some sort or you need to put in some work for me. I'll even let you pick your pleasure." I stated licking my lips.

The truth is, I wasn't even interested in having him top me off with the way he was looking and smelling today.

"Man little nigga, I'm not a fucking faggot. That shit was a onetime thing. If you think that I'm about to..."

That was all he was able to get out before his face connected with the butt of my pistol. His loud scream echoed throughout my trap house. As I was about to crack him upside his head again, I stopped when he fell to his knees and begged me not to hit him again. Maybe I was getting soft because my rage and desire to beat some respect into his stupid ass disappeared as quickly as it had surfaced.

Stooping down in front of his bloody face I coldly replied, "You better not ever fix your crack pipe smoking lips to come at me sideways. Never bite the hand that feeds you bitch! You still don't get it. You will do whatever I tell your funky ass to do! You got that nigga?!"

I paused, waiting until he nodded his head acknowledging that he understood before proceeding.

"I need you to do me a favor. This shit is very important. In fact, so important that I will kill your junky ass if you screw it up." I glared at him for a moment, waiting for him to grasp the significance of my words.

"There is this heavy hitter named Big E. All I need you to do is put your ears to the streets. Find out as much as you can about him and his bitch. I want home addresses, government names, hang out spots, hell I even want to know how often that nigga takes a shit. You got that?!" I asked poking him in his bony ribs.

He winced a little before nodding. "So, youngster, when will you take care of me? Please don't make me wait until this job is done! I won't make it!" He fearfully exclaimed.

I threw my head back and belted out a hearty laugh. "I swear, you base-heads have to be some of the most entitled sons of bitches that I've ever encountered. You bitches expect to receive payment before completing your damn jobs! Where in the fuck do they do that at?!

Here's how this little job is going to work. I will give you some work now to calm your ugly ass down. I need you to be able to function and you can't do that fiending and shit. Then you will only receive a fix upon delivering me some news that I can use. Come to me with some bullshit and I will fuck you up. Oh yeah, should your dumb ass be discovered somehow, my name better not ever escape through those crusty ass lips of yours. If they do, consider it suicide. Now get the fuck out of here and fix yourself up a little. Don't ever come in here like this again. You're making the block hot nigga." I said dismissively.

"Thank you! Thank you, man!!!" He said scurrying out of the trap house with some of my work.

∞

Over the next few weeks Mr. Berry had proved himself to be extremely useful to me. He had managed to find out where Big E laid his big ass dome, Ms. Mocha's government name, both of their hang out spots and also that Big E took approximately two shits a day. You gotta admire a nigga who is regular in the bowel department.

I only had to fuck Mr. Berry up a couple of times for coming to me with dead ends. He eventually got the point and came to me with only relevant information. Once I felt that I had received all the important information that I felt I needed, Mr. Berry's services were no longer needed.

One day, I was driving down Sullivan Ave checking up on some of my workers and trap houses when I noticed one of my goons holding a gun to Mr. B's head. Upon discovering my car, Mr. Berry instantly yelled out my name and begged me to come to his rescue. I shook my head as I chuckled to myself. My new worker Keyvon, was a beast! He didn't play around with the fiends. He was about his business and never played around when it came to the money.

I had to constantly remind his young hotheaded ass that if he murked all of our customers then there would be no money to be made. I was no pussy, but I believed in displaying some decent customer service skills with our fiends. Besides, no one was going to be killing Mr. Berry...except me. I didn't go through all of this shit just to let this young nigga swoop in and off him.

Walking up to Mr. B and Keyvon I inquired, "Yo, what seems to be the problem Von? You can't be out here in broad daylight doing shit like this man. I done told you that shit one too many times. You're making shit hot man."

"Man Luke, this bum as nigga came to me trying to cop some work from me with these counterfeit ass bills. Look at that shit boss man! He got away with it the first time. I couldn't pinpoint which fiend got me last time. I never said shit to you about it, I just replaced the loss with my own money. I went out and bought a marker that detects counterfeit money. All the money has been legit until this muthafucka came back today trying to get over again. Let me murk this fool!"

Glaring at Mr. Berry, I replied with clenched teeth, "Naw stand down. Right now, isn't the time or the place. I'll take care of this nigga myself. Let him..."

"Yo what the fuck you mean! This nigga done okie doked your ass once and tried to do it again! If you allow him to keep breathing, soon all of these fucking cluckers will think you're a joke and try you. Be smart..." He ranted as I sent off two hot ones to his heart.

I was crushed because I knew that young muthafucka was

speaking nothing but the truth. He had so much potential with my team. He was smart, dependable and his money was always on point. Unfortunately, he was too smart for his own good. I had to make a quick executive decision. As bad as I enjoyed having Keyvon working for me, I knew that he would have lost all respect for me for allowing Mr. Berry to walk.

There was no way of him knowing Mr. Berry's significance to me and my future plans with him. Nonetheless I didn't feel the need to explain myself to him either. As much as I hated killing him, I still needed Mr. Berry alive. Even more than I needed Keyvon to live at this time. Looking towards the trap house, I noticed another one of my workers, JT looking in our direction. I simply gave him a head nod ordering him to clean up the mess in the yard.

"Get your stupid ass up!" I spat at Mr. Berry.

He looked terrified but quickly jumped to his feet and followed me to my car. I opened the trunk and ordered, "Get your ass in!"

I could tell he didn't want to get into my trunk, but was afraid to challenge me. Fuck him, he wasn't getting his funky ass into my car. I hoped he was comfortable because I had several other errands to run before I reached my final destination.

∞

"Wake your ass up and you better not have pissed in my trunk either!" I yelled inspecting my car. I was surprised that he hadn't urinated in the trunk since he'd been in the hot trunk for over six hours. He looked weak, hot and dehydrated.

"Hurry up and get the hell out of my car!" He slowly sat up and looked around at his surroundings.

Growing impatient, I roughly grabbed him by the collar of his filthy shirt and tossed him onto the pavement. He yelped in pain, but I had no sympathy for his ass. He had forced me to have to kill one of my best workers and for that he was going to pay. I wasn't going to kill him; however, he was surely going to wish that I had.

"Get up and walk bitch! I know you don't think that I'm going to carry yo ass over the threshold!" I snapped.

He shakily stood up and faced me. "Walk." I ordered.

Once making it on the inside of my newly acquired building, I quickly pulled my gun out and asked Mr. Berry to give me a reason why I shouldn't blow his fucking brains out.

After listening to his bullshit reasons and excuses for a while I told him, "You stink! The smell of you is making me sick to my stomach. Take your ass into the bathroom down the hall and on the right. Take a shower, shave and throw those rags into the trash! I have new clothes in the bathroom closet. Put on something from in there."

Damn near an hour later, Mr. Berry resurfaced looking like a completely different person. Like his old self, except I could tell he was jonsing and needed to get high.

"Well I'll be damned! Who knew you could still clean up like this. You almost look normal." I joked.

He nervously laughed as he scratched his tracked-up arms. I knew he was probably too afraid to ask me for any dope so I took it upon myself to make him an offer he couldn't refuse.

"I see you over there looking as if you could use little *medicine*. Am I right?" I asked knowingly.

"Yes! Yes, man. I really need something right now. I'm hurting over here." Mr. Berry confirmed.

"Do you have any real money? Excluding that counterfeit shit?"

He sadly shook his head no.

"Well you know that you're going to have to put in work for me, right? I asked.

"Yes, young blood. Do you need me to spy on someone else for you? That's no problem. I got you!"

"No, not this time. Now listen carefully. Know that if you say no to this next job, I will kill you and then I'll kill your daughter...Gladys, right?"

I watched his eyes grow wide with fear at the mention of his daughter's name.

"Are we on the same page?" I questioned.

"Yes...please. I need something quickly." He pleaded.

"This time I'm not paying up until the job is finished."

"Oh no, don't do that to me! I'll die for sure. Please, son help me!"

I barked, "Muthafucka, I've already told you that you aren't my fucking father so stop calling me that shit! As for the job, I want to break your back-door in. What do you say?"

He was quiet for a few moments as he allowed my request to sink in. I watched as the color left his face. I could tell that he didn't want to agree, but he also knew what was at stake. He knew I meant business too. I wasn't taking 'no' for an answer today. In all honesty, his time should have been up earlier that day instead of Von.

"I find it almost amusing that you assume that I have nothing better to do than to wait on your crusty ass. What's it gonna be old man?" I said growing impatient.

"Okay, I'll do it. Just please leave my daughter out of this shit. She's innocent."

"You have my word. I will not touch a hair on her pretty head if you do what I've asked." I lied.

"I'm not gay, but what other choices do I have?" He replied sadly.

"Muthafucka I'm not gay either and you're right...you have no other alternatives. Well, besides death of course."

"Strip." I demanded.

I looked on as he slowly began to remove the clothing I'd lent him, one article at a time. Damn, Mr. B's base-head ass had it going on underneath those clothes. His body was still tight and chiseled. Once he and I were both completely naked, I told him to follow me over to the leather futon that I had in the room.

Normally, I preferred to fuck muthafuckas in the doggie-style position, however, I wanted to monitor his face as I popped his cherry. I roughly shoved him onto the futon. I was about to release all of my anger, frustrations and hatred for him through his asshole. Today I would show him no mercy. I had even opted against using my spit to lubricate his virgin hole. He was about to take this dick rough...and dry.

As he laid onto his back, he tightly closed his eyes I guess in an attempt to block out what was about to transpire. I smelled his fear and it instantly caused my pipe to stiffen up. I positioned myself between his legs and placed the head of my dick up against his asshole. I smile internally as I literally felt his asshole quiver and tighten up.

If he couldn't tolerate his asshole simply being touched, I knew I was about to have his ass screaming momentarily.

"Nigga stay still and try to relax...for your sake!" I barked mushing him in his head.

He simply nodded as he sucked in a few quick breaths. Again, placing my dick against his ass, I slowly begin pushing his tight walls aside.

He started screaming like the bitch he was while backing away from me. All bullshit aside, the head wasn't even in! I somehow managed to pin him in place beneath me. He wasn't going to be able to move anymore. It was then that I finally made my way all the way inside of him. I watched as fresh tears begin to stream down his snitching ass face.

"Ahhhhhhhh! Come on man! You've made your poooiinnnt!!! Ooooooooh this shit hurts nigga! I can't stand this shit anymore! No more. Please have mercy youngster. No more!!! Ahhhhhhhh!!!!!!" He cried as he attempted to push me off him.

Nothing but death would've made me stop at that moment. I two-pieced his cry baby ass and said, "Muthafucka, I told you to stay still! I ain't stopping until I get my nut! Unfortunately for you, I don't plan on cumming anytime soon. I'm thoroughly enjoying myself right now."

I never even missed a stroke throughout my speech. This only made me pick up my pace. Soon I was pummeling him.

I had blacked out at some point because glancing at my

watch forty-five minutes later, I was drenched in sweat yet still going to town. Looking down at his ass, he appeared to be dead. I slowed down my stroke...but didn't stop so that I could assess his breathing.

I breathe a sigh of relief as I watch his chest rise and fall. His weak ass must've blacked out as well from the pain. Glancing at my dick and his asshole I saw exactly why this nigga was out. I had ripped his asshole open to the white meat. I was no doctor but any fool could see that he was going to need several stitches to close him back up. Blood was all over the both of us but I refused to let that interrupt my growing nut.

Roughly slapping Mr. Berry awake I said, "Hey bitch, wake up! You're about to miss the grand finale!"

I was so excited that spittle flew from my mouth and landed on his face. Once I had his attention I jack hammered his tender hole as he howled for mercy.

Feeling the point of no return approaching I yelled, "Fuuuuucccckkkkk!!! Fuuuuucccckkkkk!!!"

My body jerked as I plunged deep inside of Mr. B one last time before I shot my load into his bloody asshole.

I was spent, but it was time for his crack-headed ass to roll out.

"Aye, aye bitch. Here take this shit and get the fuck out of here!" I yelled throwing him a small package of his drug of choice.

Although I knew he was in pain by his facial expressions and movements, he hurriedly dressed and damn near ran out of my building. Locking the door behind him, I dashed into the bathroom to wash that nigga's blood and scent off me. In the shower, I did a victory dance knowing I had taken that bastard's cherry. Next stop...his daughter, Gladys.

« Chapter 16 Paid In Full »

The Past "Lukas"

PRIDE IS A POWERFUL thing. As bad as I wanted to reach out to Gladys, my pride prevented me from doing so. The streets talked so I'd been hearing about her running around with some lame ass college nigga. Deep down I knew she was better off without me in her life, yet I still wanted her for myself. I made a vow to myself, when I was ready for her, nothing or no one was going to stop me from stepping back into that number one spot.

Prior to Mr. B's death, he had provided me with lots of useful information regarding Big E and Ms. Mocha. Her government name was actually Serenity. It had been over a year since my trip to Dallas and also since Mr. Berry had died. I finally decided to check up on the lovely pair to see if I could snatch her away from him. That bitch was worth the price of at least five basic bitches!

I'd found out that she was now pregnant with their first child and that they'd been together for three years. Although she was in her ninth month of pregnancy, she was still one of the baddest females I'd ever laid eyes on. She exuded sex appeal. I had followed Serenity and Big E around for weeks undetected and I could tell they were in love. It wouldn't be easy prying her away from his yellow ass. He rarely left her side.

One evening while following them, we ended up right in front of what was then called St. John's Mercy Hospital. I watched as Big E jumped his big ass out and ran over to the passenger side of his truck and assisted her out. She appeared to be in excruciating pain as he cradled her into his arms like a baby so that she wouldn't have to walk from the parking garage.

I made a mental note to leave her alone for a month or two in order to heal. Then it was going to be time for her to get to work. I had waited long enough. Slowly driving off, I nearly salivated at the thought of all the money she'd eventually bring me.

∞

After leaving the hospital last night, I had an extremely profitable night. I had managed to lure in two dime pieces. They weren't on Gladys or Serenity's level, but I had received twenty-five thousand for each of them. I couldn't complain. Today I had a lot to do. I was finally registering for classes at UMSL. I had decided that obtaining my MBA would help me a lot with all my prospective business ventures. It was also to show G that I was serious about us.

I knew this entire college ordeal was going to feel so strange...mostly because I would be much older than the other students. I was a smart guy so I wasn't worried about my academics. I never realized what a pain registering for school would be. I felt as if I were sent to a dozen different offices and waiting areas. The lines were always longer than a Section 8 waiting list. I was annoyed, hungry and my dogs were barking.

The gleeful chatter of the other young students got under my skin. I was pleased to have avoided the ridiculously long line that contained the financial aid recipients. I didn't need any charity. I had brought the fifty G's that I earned last night and I knew that should be more than enough to pay for my first year of college.

"Okay Mr. Monroe, your projected balance for your first year is $17,495. You do not have to pay that now, the total balance for this semes..." The elderly registrar stated.

Cutting her off I responded, "No ma'am, I'd like to just pay my tuition up for the year and have it over and done with. I would like to avoid having to sit through this circus for a while if you don't mind."

Lightly chuckling she responded, "That's completely understandable. Are you receiving any grants, loans or scholarships?"

Shaking my head I pulled open my black ferragamo revival briefcase. I was looking and feeling like a million bucks. The fifty thousand dollars was separated into stacks of one thousand dollars to make the process of counting easier. I handed her seventeen stacks and five crisp one hundred dollar bills. "Here you go ma'am." I replied with a smile showcasing my pearly whites.

Her eyes were opened so widely that I thought them muthafuckas were about to roll out onto her cheap ass desk. "Wow! I've been doing this for over thirty years and I can honestly say that no one has ever paid this amount in cash before. They've written checks for this amount but have never paid in cash."

"Well Miss, they say you learn and see something new every day. I hate the thought of loans lingering out there accruing interest."

"That's very smart thinking young man. Here is your receipt and change sir and I wish you the best of luck with your studies." She gave me a genuine smile that reached her eyes.

"I appreciate that. Thank you." I said as I retrieved the remaining five hundred dollars from my stack and laid it on her desk. "Here, treat yourself to something nice ma'am."

Before she could protest, I was already out of her office with all of my registration papers in my briefcase. In those days, that was a lot of money! I had opted to attend full-time which consisted of four classes. I prayed that I didn't bite off more than I could chew. I hadn't been in school for over twelve years. Truth be told, I only went then to make my money. That was of course before Mr. Berry had me expelled with his funky ass.

I had gone back and achieved my GED. It wasn't as good as a high school diploma, but given my circumstances it had to suffice. Walking back to my car I felt such a sense of accomplishment. Although all I'd done today was register for my classes, I somehow felt even more powerful than I typically did.

I felt like celebrating and I wanted nothing more than to run to Gladys and tell her that I was becoming who she wanted me to be. However I nixed that notion. I knew that I had a long way to go and several changes to make before I stepped to her. I'm not going to lie, I missed the fuck out of her ass.

"Fuck it." I mumbled to myself as I proceeded to follow one of the loud talking student's from the registration office. She wasn't a dime, but I was pretty sure that she'd replace the money I'd just spent. Hell, someone had to pay for my college tuition...I sure in the fuck wasn't!

« Chapter 17 The Magician »

The Past "Gladys"

THEY SAY GOD NEVER puts more on us than we can bear. The funny thing is, most people rarely find comfort in that saying while in the midst of their unhappiness. I was approaching the fifth month of my pregnancy and Omar had all but disappeared from my life. After the ER doctor congratulated me on my unexpected pregnancy, I hadn't seen Omar anymore.

The bastard was the one who had driven me the ER yet he'd left me stranded there after he discovered I was pregnant. Upon my discharge, I had my nurse call me a cab. I headed straight to my family home to find that he had packed his belongings and left. I hadn't felt this empty since my dad died or since I made the decision to erase Lukas from my life.

I felt completely alone. Of course I had Paige and I had my church friends, but I needed a father for my baby. As I lay on my living room couch, I alternated between crying and praying. I knew God had bigger plans for me than single motherhood. I deserved better. Then again, this could be my punishment for having premarital sex.

I knew better than to question God. I trusted him and knew that I was meant to have my baby. I prayed that Omar would come to see our baby as the blessing that he or she truly was. I'd concluded that he just needed time to adjust to the surprising revelation.

"He'll come around." I mumbled to myself before drifting off to a tearful sleep.

∞

That was five months ago and he still hadn't come around. After attempting to track him down endlessly for weeks, I'd finally given up. I was too busy with my studies to chase a man who didn't want to be caught. Paige was a true Godsend. Although I had plenty of money saved, she always insisted on giving me money to set aside for the baby or was always walking in with baby clothes and toys.

She accompanied me to all my appointments and ensured that I took my prenatal vitamins every day. She was convinced that I was having a girl and had even named her Celeste. I really wanted a boy so that I could name him Dante' after my late father. It was settled. She'd name the girl and I'd name the boy.

School was going well. I was picking up heavy loads in hopes that it would lessen the overall time before I graduated. Don't get me wrong I loved school, but I was eager to finish so that I could finally fulfill my passion to teach. I was still a waitress and although I enjoyed it for the most part, I couldn't wait to retire my apron. During the time I'd spent waitressing, I had grown a new found respect for the hard work they did. They were certainly unappreciated and underpaid.

Finally reaching my seventh month of pregnancy, I found myself nesting like crazy. I had become more of a perfectionist and wanted everything to be just right for when I delivered my baby. I had decided that I'd move back into my family home after I delivered my baby.

Although Paige begged me not to leave, I was almost certain that I'd have no choice either way due to the campus policies. I told her that she was welcome to move into one of my rooms if she wanted to. I reasoned that she could then use our dorm room for her side "hustle".

She declined my offer because she didn't want to intrude or be that far away from campus which was understandable. I was personally going to miss being so close to the school myself.

One Saturday morning I decided to go to Walgreens to pick up a new razor, some cocoa butter, nail polish and Dove body wash. I routinely inspected my skin praying that I didn't get any of those horrible looking stretch marks on my body. That was one of my biggest fears. I was always very careful not to scratch my stomach, sides or lower back. I was now a compulsive shaver as well. I refused to deliver my baby and be caught off guard with hairy legs and a hairy kitty. No ma'am!

Like most women, I always came out of stores with so much more than I initially went in for. Loading four overstuffed bags into my trunk, I was startled by someone softly tapping me on my left shoulder. I nearly pissed on myself! My bladder certainly wasn't what it used to be.

Quickly turning around, I saw none other than the magician...Omar. He pulled disappearing acts like no other! He was better than Houdini himself! He was as handsome as I remembered, but that no longer mattered to me. I no longer wanted anything to do with him. I just wanted him to step up and be there for our child.

He was silent, but his wide eyes were intensely fixated on my swollen midsection. I appeared to be carrying twins. Scratch that...triplets! As pissed with him as I had been, I couldn't help but to be embarrassed in front of him. Here he was looking like a chocolate snack and I was standing here looking as if I had eaten them all. My nose was super wide and my summer dress had a large mustard stain on it from the two Quik-Trip hotdogs I'd scarfed down earlier in the car.

I was painfully aware that I had been caught off my game. My eyes lowered to the ground. I noticed my puffy feet struggling to free themselves from the tight straps of my sandals. No wonder he ditched me. I'm a hot mess! I thought to myself.

Hot tears began to stream down my face. I was so disappointed in him. His disappearing act had hurt me to the core. I had given him parts of me that no other guy had been lucky enough to receive, yet he'd still discarded me like a piece of trash. I deserved better than what he had done to me. I stood in the parking lot of that Wal-greens sobbing like a raving lunatic.

At some point he silently embraced me in his arms and allowed me to saturate his shirt with my liquid sorrow. I had previously played out so many scenarios of how I'd conduct myself in his presence when I finally caught up with him. I'll be honest, this didn't occur in any of those scenarios. I thought I'd be much stronger than this. I didn't curse, but I thought I would whenever we reconnected.

I was an emotional wreck and didn't realize just how much I truly missed him until this very moment. I was so humbled and grateful to finally be around him that I didn't even entertain anger. Our baby must have felt 'his' dad's presence because 'he' was super active.

"Gladys, I am so sorry for leaving. I have no right to ask you this, but do you think you could ever forgive me? I was scared. Terrified! I didn't think that I could handle this. By the time I figured out I could, I was too ashamed to face you. I was a coward and I know it. You look so damn beautiful carrying my child.

You're absolutely glowing. Do you think we can go someplace and talk?" He asked.

After crying as much as I had, all I could do was nod my head yes. I told him that I still had some errands to run, but I would cook dinner later and we could talk then.

∞

Later that evening I was putting the finishing touches on my makeup. I don't know why I even bothered. He didn't deserve the effort that I'd gone through this evening to get ready. Silly me. I had even picked up a new maternity outfit to wear tonight from an expensive boutique.

I had cooked lamb, asparagus and homemade garlic potatoes. For dessert, I had baked a deliciously moist red velvet cake. The amazing aromas permeating throughout my house had my stomach growling. I had toyed with the idea of starting dinner without him several times. Just as I was about to take a huge bite out of the lamb, I heard my doorbell ring.

Rolling my eyes, I slowly backed away from the stove. As I nervously approached the front door I plastered a big smile on my face. Swinging the door open, my mouth dropped open at the sight of how amazing Omar looked. Oh and he smelled even more delicious than the meal I'd just prepared.

My body had craved him throughout my entire pregnancy. I yearned for his touch and intimacy. As he embraced me in his strong arms, I felt my lower lips become glossy. I hated that he had this effect on me. Hell, he and I both knew his sex was wack! So why did my body still respond to him this way?!

As he planted his soft lips on top of mine, I was proud of myself when I heard, "Omar, stop. This isn't what needs to happen right now. I am still working on forgiving you, however, I will *never* forget what you've done. Now if you'd like to talk, then I'm game. Don't expect anything else," escape my lips.

He appeared to be caught off guard for a moment, but simply nodded his handsome head in surrender. Releasing myself from his embrace, he proceeded to trail behind me as I made my way back into the kitchen. I made our plates and allowed him to bless our food.

He spent much of the evening apologizing, while I was merely interested in discussing how we'd coparent. What was done was done. While I loved him tremendously, I just couldn't get past everything so quickly. Maybe in due time.

« Chapter 18 Loose Flapper »

The Past "Celeste"

IT HAS BEEN FOUR MONTHS since the infamous staircase incident. Getting through therapy proved to be the most difficult time of my life. I never thought that I'd regain my strength. I was still in a great deal of pain and relied heavily on my pain medications to get me through the day. Alicia, baby Sincere and my mom had been mainstays at my bedside. Shawn and Joe called frequently to check on me.

I had successfully avoided Eli and my so-called father kept fairly distant from me. Maybe his guilty conscience had kicked in for once. My mom claimed that Mr. Monroe had entered rehab and that they both were attending counseling. My mom seemed to be genuinely trying.

I'd returned to work a week ago and it was nice to feel productive again. I'd spent so much time feeling so incredibly sorry for myself over the past few months. I don't know how, but Joe saw to it that my paychecks continued rolling in despite my absence. My savings account was looking pretty damn good.

I didn't realize how much I'd truly missed my coworkers and customers until I walked through the front door of Divas R Us. Of course, they threw me a surprise welcome back party. I'd never felt so loved. Despite everyone's protests to take it easy, I was determined to earn my keep.

In spite of my previous reservations towards both Joe and his wife, I must admit they had been angels throughout my convalescing period. They'd always show up with stuffed animals, candy, flowers and the freaking best food ever! The only odd thing is pretty much every time they visited, I would get extremely sleepy and I'd have the oddest dreams. Always sexual in nature. Perverse even. Sometimes I'd dream about the two of them having sex while Sia would go down on me. Other times I'd dream that Joe was having sex with me while Sia just stood back and watched.

The dreams at times felt so real that I'd wake up checking my vagina and underwear, but I never noticed anything unusual. Thankfully, now that I was better and back at work, the nightmares ceased.

I was still the captain of Team Fuck Eli. Initially when I returned to school, his yellow ass thought that he'd just pop up and squirm he way back into my life.

"Thank goodness Celeste! I've been coming up here every day just to see you! It is so nice to see you back at school. I've been so worried about you baby. Listen we need to ta.." Eli exclaimed before I tried my hardest to slap his conniving ass back into last week.

If looks could kill, I would've been dead ten times over. He appeared to be embarrassed and full of rage, however, I wasn't fearful of him. There wasn't a blow that he could deliver that I hadn't felt before. I humorously looked on as my handprint stained his face.

"Listen boy, I have told you before to leave me the hell alone! You graduated already, so why are you here?! We have absolutely nothing to talk about! Go talk to my *sister*! I fucking hate you. You're dead to me!" I stormed off with finality.

Since that day, he fell back. He hadn't said a single word to me, but his eyes never left me whenever we happened to cross paths. His nasty ass could look all day as long as he kept his grubby paws to himself.

My "sister" Kennedy was certainly smarter than she looked. She didn't dare fix her face to throw out her typical insults. A part of me was grateful but the other part was ready to connect her face with my fists. This year everyone seemed to want to take me out of character. I couldn't wait to finish up high school and leave this shitty town for good.

When the final bell rang releasing us for the day, I moved as quickly as my sore body would allow me to. I needed to get to my locker so that I could take some of my prescribed Percocet. It didn't seem to be helping as much as it had been in the beginning so I had to resort to taking two to three tablets at a time. At this rate, I was running out quickly and would have to have it refilled soon.

Reaching my locker I swiftly swallowed three of my pain pills without the aid of water. I prayed it would kick in fast. I had just enough pills to last me until tomorrow, so I knew I'd be stopping by the pharmacy bright and early. Today my main focus was meeting and hanging out with my neighbor Shawn.

He'd been coming home more frequently to check on me since my "accident". He was always a pleasant breath of fresh air. His goofy humor always distracted me from all of the madness of my everyday life. Shawn was majoring in history. He was so informative and knew something about everything. I've always considered myself to be an intelligent person, however, I always learned so much from Shawn whenever I was in his presence.

Although not many people knew the truth behind my mysterious fall down the stairs, Shawn immediately knew my fictitious story was bullshit. Choosing not to play with his intelligence, I told him everything. Everything included Eli's bet, him cheating on me with Kennedy, Eli stealing my car which led to me being pushed down the stairs, then finding out Kennedy was my sister and last but not least the fact that...my dad was NOT my dad.

I couldn't make shit like this up! Shawn of course wanted to kick my dad and Eli's ass. I assured him that he had too much to lose and that neither of them was worth the attention. I had survived everything and it had only made me stronger.

I didn't know how, but I felt that one day things would get much better for me. I knew that God had bigger and better plans for me than the hell that I was currently living in. I was now a senior in high school and I only needed to make it through this last year and I'd be home free. I was already incessantly filling out college applications and every college that I was interested in was hundreds of miles away from St. Louis.

Once I left St. Louis I never planned to return. The few that I loved and the few that loved me would have to meet me in Illinois because I did not want to ever cross back over the Missouri state lines. Aside from Alicia and Shawn I doubted that anyone would miss me anyway.

Upon exiting my school I saw Shawn standing near his car with a big Kool-Aid smile on his handsome face. He agreed to meet me at school and from there we would go and catch a movie. At this time of day, we'd catch a fairly cheap matinee and they wouldn't be too crowded. It was 1995 and we were having a difficult time deciding on which movie to watch. I really wanted to see Clueless, but Shawn wanted to see Friday.

After we played rock-paper-scissors several times, I was deemed the loser. This meant we ended up watching Friday. Friday turned out to be an amazingly funny movie and we had a great time. The loser, which was me, also ended up having to purchase the snacks for the winner. I humorously pretended to have an attitude the entire night. Following the movie we went to a place called Incredible Pizza in South County. Incredible Pizza was a nice little family oriented hangout. It was equivalent to an adult Chuck-E-Cheese. They had a buffet and an arcade.

Shawn and I ran around that building like two kindergarteners. I ate to the point that my pants felt as if they we're going to burst at the seams. It was the most fun I had had in a very long time. It felt great to laugh. I wish everyday could be like this one. When it was time to leave Incredible Pizza, a sudden wave of sadness washed over me. I wasn't ready for our evening to end and I damn sure didn't want to go home.

Sensing my sudden sadness Shawn inquired as to why I had such a long face. "What's wrong Celeste? I thought we were having a good time. Did I do or say something wrong?"

"Nothing. I'm okay. Let's just go." I snapped.

"What the fuck?! How many times do I have to tell you that you cannot lie to me Celeste? I know when something is bothering you. Now what's up?" Shawn questioned.

"I'm just not ready for tonight to end. I really don't want to go home." I whispered looking down at my feet.

"Then why didn't your little spoiled ass just say so. Let's find a payphone. Tell your mom that you're spending a night with Alicia. I'll rent a room, some movies and board games. Okay?" He stated lifting my chin up forcing me to make eye contact.

His honey colored eyes and dimples made me blush. When did Shawn start looking like this? I remember when he still pissed in the bed.

Finding a payphone a few blocks away from Incredible Pizza, I told my mom that Alicia was sick and needed help watching her son and twin sisters. I told her Ms. Trina was stuck at the hospital working an extra shift again. My mom agreed that it was okay if I stayed over to help out. I then phoned Alicia and filled her in on our plans. Of course her nosy ass had a million questions, but they'd have to be addressed some other time.

We then got into Shawn's car and he drove to the South County Walmart. As promised we picked up board games, snacks, pajamas, toiletries and some movies. Shawn then drove to a nearby Red Roof Inn and got us all checked in as I waited in the car. I was excited because I didn't have to go home and I would be spending more time with Shawn before he returned to school.

We took turns taking showers. We each had our own separate bed. We had selected a combination of comedy and horror movies to watch throughout the night. We both opted to watch Candyman first. This led to me hopping into Shawn's bed for protection. That movie was absolutely terrifying. He laughed at my childishness, yet he snuggled up next to me anyway. I felt so safe with his arms around me. I knew he'd kick Candyman's ass if he came after me.

After Candyman ended, we decided to lighten the mood and play a comedy. I had chosen to watch The Mask which featured Jim Carrey. I loved Jim Carrey and thought he was one of the silliest comedians out there. We were not even fifteen minutes into the movie when Shawn asked if I remembered what happened in the tree house last year.

"Of course I remember, I don't have dementia fool. What about it?" I joked.

"Well, that's the thing, I can't seem to forget. We've never had the opportunity to talk about it afterwards. I think about it all the time. I think about how great you tasted and about how fresh you smelled. Did you like it...be honest."

"Shawn I always try to be honest with you because you see right through me anyway. Honestly it was the best feeling I've ever experienced in my life, but it was also one of the most embarrassing events in my life. I was seriously laying there thinking that I was about to urinate in your mouth. I now know better and I know that I was about to have an orgasm that day. We were both idiots and had no business doing what we were doing...because we didn't *know* what we were doing." I answered honestly.

"You know a lot has changed since last year? I still haven't been with any of the women at school, but I've learned a lot from our experience that day. At this point, we've experienced all of our first together with the exception of one, how do you feel about going all the way tonight Cee Cee?" Shawn asked with a serious face.

After taking a few moments to take in what he'd just asked me, I replied, "Shawn, I cannot think of anyone else I'd rather share that experience with. Fuck it, let's do!" I bravely boasted.

Not skipping a beat, Shawn immediately removed his shirt followed by his pants. He was down to his boxers and peering at me longingly. Catching the hint, I too begin to remove my shirt followed by my pants. I was clad only in my bra and panties. Our goofy asses just looked at one another for a while kind of at a loss as to what to do next.

Out of nowhere, a sense of boldness took over me. I leaned into him, connecting his lips with mine. He appeared to be caught off guard for a moment, but he soon matched me as our tongues wrestled together. Shawn turned me on so much. The way my body responded to his touch scared me to death. He was bringing about feelings and sensations that I never thought he'd be capable of doing. After all, this was just my silly next door neighbor who I've known all my life.

Pushing Shawn onto his back, I swiftly removed my bra in one smooth motion. I then climbed on top of him. As I straddled him, I started to slow grind to imaginary music. I could feel so much of him through the thin material of my panties as well as his boxers. There was so much heat permeating from between my thighs, that I thought I was about to create fire. I leaned forward so that his mouth would have full access to feast on my breasts. He needed no invitations.

He smashed both of my tits together and attempted to stuff them both into his mouth. I was pretty damn impressed.

Flipping me over, he decided to take control. He excitedly pulled my drenched panties off.

"Cee Cee, if you don't mind, I'd like to skip the foreplay for now. I just want to feel you right now. I've been waiting years for this. I'll take care of you later. I promise, you know that I'm good for it. We have the room all night." He assured me.

Understanding where he was coming from, I simply nodded.

Leaning over to pick up his pants, he reached into one of the pockets and extracted a small box of condoms. I smirked because he came prepared for tonight. I watched as he opened up the packaging and wrapper. He then clumsily applied the condom down onto the shaft of his penis. He was a nice size, but not too big. Parting my knees with his, Shawn immediately pressed himself into me.

To my surprise, he slid right in with minimal effort. There was absolutely no pain. The shit felt great! He appeared stunned too for a moment, but pleasure soon claimed his face. The first time he last a good two minutes, however, he rocked back up for round two. This time I climbed on top of him. I rode him as if my life depended on it...for about one and a half minutes before he again succumbed to my sugar walls.

He was determined to last five minutes as he slid on the final condom and bent me over. He plowed into me with so much force that I finally cried out in pain. His door knockers were somehow tapping up against my pearl as I moaned into the pillow. Just as I was about to cum, he blew his load again at the two minute mark.

Although we'd been sexing for less than ten minutes we were both spent and ready to call it a night.

Preparing for a night of cuddling, I wrapped my arm and leg around Shawn who already had his back towards me. He quickly knocked both my arm and leg off him.

"Celeste, you're foul as shit. Did you seriously think that I was gonna believe that you were a virgin with that loose ass flapper?! I mean, don't get me wrong...the pussy is good. But you are certainly *not* a virgin. Who the hell did you fuck Cee Cee? And don't you dare lie to me!" He snarled.

I couldn't help but to burst into tears. Why was he being so mean to me? I thought we'd had a good time and now he was being a complete dick to me.

"Shawn, I swear, I have never been with anyone else before tonight. I only allowed Eli to eat me out that one time I told you about earlier. Remember?" I reminded him.

"Man, get the fuck out of here with that Cee Cee. Get the hell out of my bed. Go sleep in your own bed. I gave myself to a lying ass whore. I thought we were giving each other, to one another. You disgust me. Move!" He yelled loudly.

I took off towards my purse and grabbed four Percocets from the bottle. I hurriedly swallowed them before quietly crying myself to sleep. Too bad I didn't have a full bottle otherwise I would've consumed them all. What was Shawn tripping about? I *was* a virgin...what the fuck was going on?!

« Chapter 19 Six Is Company »

The Past "Mike"

IT TOOK EVERYTHING WITHIN me not to put a bullet between Shay's eyes. As I drove back to the warehouse I seethed as I internally cursed her the fuck out. Once my adrenaline wore off, I realized that she had truly fucked me up! My nose certainly wasn't broken, however, it had yet to stop leaking blood all over my four hundred dollar shirt. That bitch was a true fighter...a survivor. If under different circumstances, I could've used her on the streets. She had potential, but unfortunately she'd never live long enough to explore those options.

Pulling up to the warehouse, I grew excited as I thought about how taking care of these two bitches would result in me getting my family back. They were sacrificing themselves for the greater good...so to speak.

As I got out of my car and walked towards the trunk, I got my knife ready just in case Shay had woken her super strong ass up and was feeling froggy. Cautiously popping the trunk open, I was satisfied to discover a sleeping Shay. I loved when I used the right amount of chloroform. Not taking any chances, I hog tied and carried her into the warehouse.

Once inside, I immediately noticed Tamar glaring at me from across the room. After securing Shay to her chair, I walked over to Tamar.

"Why T, what possessed you to do something like that? How could you, a mother, do something like that to another mother? I'm having a difficult time understanding how you could do some shit like this not only to my girl, but to my son! And you claim that you love me! Can't live without me! That shit wasn't love!" I yelled as tears of frustration trickled down my cheeks.

I didn't care if she saw me cry because she'd never live long enough to tell anyone about it. I cried because I hated how her selfish act was about to force me to kill her. No matter how much I tried to convince myself that she was this big, bad monster, I knew she was the same beautiful Tamar that I had grown to care about.

As much as I didn't want to take her out, I knew it was the only way to salvage my family. After I stopped yelling, I watched tears flood Tamar's face as well.

"Baby, I'm so sorry for what we've done." She stated, motioning between her and Shay.

She continued, "I just could not handle the thought of another woman carrying your baby...especially your son! I was supposed to have your first son! I love you so much that sometimes it makes me insane. When I saw your precious Alicia in the park that day...something in me just snapped! It wasn't premeditated...I swear to you.

I coincidentally happened to be at the park trying to walk off some of my baby weight and Shay was there for motivation. You know she is a personal trainer. Mike baby, please forgive me. I'm so sorry for all the chaos that has resulted from my actions. Please don't kill us. I've learned my lesson! Look at what you've already done to my fingers! Enough is enough!"

Damn, I had almost forgotten that I'd cut her fingers off and burned her ass with my blunt. I was definitely in my zone earlier. Now I actually felt bad seeing how pitiful and in pain she was. I wanted to comfort her, but I had to remind myself that she almost killed Alicia and my son. There was just no justifying that shit.

Staring into my face, I could tell she was attempting to see if she had somehow managed to convince me not to kill them. I got my emotions under control and now sported my best poker face. Deciding to make her squirm, I turned on my heels and left the room without a word. Hell, I still needed that shower!

∞

"Rise and shine bitches!!!" I yelled pouring a bucket of ice cold water into both of their faces. Their startled screams sent me into a fit of laughter. I had never witnessed anyone's eyes open so quickly. Since their hands were tied, they couldn't even wipe the water from their eyes. It took them both a few moments to focus in on me and when they did, of course Tamar was their honorary spokesperson.

"What the fuck Mike! Your black ass plays too damn much! Let us go already! I need to get to the damn hospital! My arms are starting to feel numb." Tamar whined.

"Hey bitch, would you like some cheese with that 'whine'? This isn't Burger King muthafucka...shit is only going *my* way around here!" I said jokingly, but was dead serious.

We were interrupted by loud knocks on the warehouse door. Looking into their direction I smiled as I went to open the door.

"By the way, Shay, you have company Ma." I said as I opened the heavy door.

Stepping back, I watched as six of my homies from around the way walked in. Some I had even played ball with over the years. Once inside, I thought I'd be a somewhat decent host and make proper introductions.

"Hey Shay, I want you to meet my brothers from several different mothers. That's Dice, Redd, BJ, Smooth, Playboy and Sammy," I exclaimed pointing to each of them with a nod of my head.

"Fellas, this is Shay. I told you all about her. Apparently, she is into that rough shit. I hope that you thoroughly enjoy yourselves, but be careful. She is much stronger than she looks, if you know what I mean!" I said grabbing my crotch with a smile.

This caused them to release excited chuckles. Their excitement had me smiling on the inside too. They were looking super thirsty right now. They were like deprived dogs, waiting to sink their teeth into a meal. Both Tamar and Shay's eyes were as big as half-dollars.

I don't know why T was looking worried, she was safe. I had already told those niggas that it was lights out if they even looked her way. True, I had issued the bitch a death sentence, yet in the meantime, she was *still* my bitch. Wasn't anyone tapping that shit. Shay was a different story. I'm not going to lie, my ass got curious a few hours ago and decided to see how she worked her little pussy. That shit was great! I made Tamar's dumb ass watch too.

Glancing around the room at my homies disrobing, I was happy that I'd already gotten my chance to beat Shay's cookie up. Hell, once those niggas finished with her, I was one-hundred percent sure that she would be void of any walls in the near future.

"Rest in peace good pussy," I stated seriously while taking

my index finger and drawing an imaginary crucifix across my chest.

Not wanting to miss a minute of the show, I grabbed a chair and sat next to my sobbing baby momma.

"Damn, T, I should've made some popcorn. Do you want some popcorn?" I inquired.

She sadly and hesitantly nodded her head yes. I knew she wanted to say no out of respect for her friend, but I also knew that she had to be starving. Quickly running to the back, I made the popcorn and I ran back in the nick of time. I had to feed Tamar because I still had her arms tied and I knew she wouldn't be able to pick up the popcorn with her little nubs anyway.

Looking at my homies in action, I almost felt sorry for the bitch. They were wearing her ass out! That bitch literally had a dick in every orifice in her body. Redd's dumbass was even trying to fuck the bend of the hoe's right knee! Those fools were wild as fuck. Shay was screaming at the top of her lungs, around the dick in her mouth for them to have mercy.

Eventually she quieted down and only an occasional whimper could be heard. That shit was so brutal that after a while I had to turn me and Tamar's chairs around. Finally after three hours, all seven of their asses were sweaty, stinking and spent.

My homies all thanked me for my generosity and told me to call them to entertain Shay again soon. I told them they could come back as often as they liked, but they'd have to pay. Today was just a little sampler. They told me that they'd be back tomorrow with the money and possibly a few extra guys.

I made it clear that I didn't give a fuck who came to fuck

her, I just needed five-hundred a head. They all had money to spend so they didn't even bat an eye. This bitch was lucky. Her pussy was saving her life at the moment. I guess I'd let her breath for another week or so. Glancing at Tamar, I still hadn't figured out what to do with her yet. Damn! Why did I have to love this bitch too?!

« Chapter 20 Channel Two »

The Past "Alicia"

I'D DECIDED TO LEAVE Sincere with my mom while I stopped by the bank to return the remainder of Ape man's money. I was still so annoyed by the entire ordeal. I could think of dozens of other things I could be doing other than entertaining this fool.

I had called Noel about two hours ago and we had agreed to meet at the same Wal-Mart in order for me to return the rest of his money. I was dressed casually in white fitted jeans and a pink spaghetti strap shirt. My short hair was curled to perfection. My face was free from makeup with the exception of lip gloss and mascara. I hadn't figured out how to cover the cut on my cheek so I spent a great deal of my time covering it with my hand or looking down.

Walking towards the entrance, I immediately recognize a familiarly unattractive face. I grimaced as his features came more into focus with each step I took in his direction. He was grinning from ear to ear and genuinely appeared happy to see me. He reached his arms out as if he were expecting a hug. Instead of walking into his embrace, I suspiciously looked him up and down.

I didn't know his ass like that to be hugging and shit. He didn't seem offended by the rejection. His smile never wavered; however, he did lower his arms.

"Good afternoon Noel. Again, I totally appreciate the kind gesture. Here is the rest of your money...two-hundred and twelve dollars. You're welcome to count it if you like." I stated.

That seemed to annoy him slightly.

"Now Alicia, do I really seem like the type of person that would be hurting over two hundred funky dollars. I could care less about the bread I spent on you. There is a lot more where that came from shorty. I honestly saw you and couldn't take my eyes off of you yesterday. You are absolutely stunning. I would love to be given the time to get to know you better.

I'm not an idiot and neither am I blind. I know you are way out of my league in the looks department, however, you will experience nothing but happy days if you give me a chance to show you. I promise, you wouldn't regret it." Noel professed sincerely.

I couldn't help but to look down at the grown. I was suddenly self-conscious of that ugly cut on my face and felt inferior to his powerful presence.

Gently lifting my face up with his index finger he replied, "I don't care about that little scratch on your face shorty. You are still one of the baddest women I've seen in a long time. Hold your head up gorgeous. I'm ugly as hell and you couldn't pay me not to hold my head up high, ya dig?"

I slowly nodded my head. He seemed to be reading my every thought. I had never seen anyone with his level of confidence before. It was so alluring.

"Look Noel, I just got out of a crappy relationship. Also, just in case you didn't notice, I have a baby. You seem like a genuinely nice guy...I'm just not ready to start dating again. I'm still in high school and not really sure of my future. I have nothing to offer you." I replied sadly.

"Alicia, what did he do to you?! I don't even know you but I can tell that you have a lot to offer. Having a baby isn't the end of the world. I met little man and I'd love to get to know him better too. I'm willing to take it slow and allow time for you to mend your heart, but I want you. Just let me take you out on one date and if you still aren't feeling me, I'll leave you alone for good. Deal?"

I studied his face for a moment. I looked into his eyes and tried to determine if he was sincere or not. I then thought about Mike and then Sincere. I had a new baby and a psychotic baby daddy on the loose. What would happen if it got back to Mike? St. Louis was very small and everyone knew everyone.

"Do we have a deal?" He repeated interrupting my thoughts.

"I'm afraid Noel. If my son's father found out, he'd hurt both of us..."

"Do I look the least bit worried baby girl? Excuse my language but screw him. I'll always protect you from him and everyone else if you allow me to. So what's it going to be?"

I don't know why, but I felt that I could trust Noel. He seemed like a genuinely good guy. He even seemed less...ugly to me. His spirit, personality and confidence made him beautiful.

"Okay Noel. Just one date. We have to be extremely careful because this cannot get back to Mike. You do not know him the way that I know him."

"Again, Mike does not move me. My only concern is getting to know you and my future stepson. To know me is to love me. You will love me one day. I know it. Mark my words gorgeous. I'm going to pick you up Saturday at seven. Get grown and sexy for me okay?"

"I got you Noel. I will call you later with the address okay?" I promised.

∞

I was sitting on the couch feeding Sincere when the phone started ringing. Slowly getting up, I walked over to the phone and picked up the receiver.

"Hello." I answered.

"Sis! Turn your tv on to the channel two news now!" An excited Cee Cee yelled.

"Okay, okay," I said placing Sincere up to my chest preparing to burp him.

I picked up the remote and did as I was told. I drew in a surprised breath as I saw photos of Sha'Keisha's ugly ass across my tv screen. Apparently she had been beaten into a coma and had finally succumbed to her injuries. While I was not fan of hers, I certainly would never wish a brutal end like that on anyone.

"Alicia, girl are you still there?!" I heard through the receiver.

Snapping my open mouth shut, I came out of my temporary trance.

"Yes, I just can't believe it! What the hell happened to her?" I inquired.

"They aren't sure really. She was found beaten to a bloody pulp in front of the White Castle on North Linbergh. It is unclear if the attack happened there or if it was just the drop off spot."

"This is crazy. Life is so short. You just never know when your number is up Cee Cee. Who would do something like that? Do you think..."

"Girl hell no! Not even Mike is that crazy! I bet she just got caught up messing with the wrong chick's man. Not everyone is willing to just walk away nowadays. These heifers are serious about these deadbeat ass men out here." Celeste hypothesized.

"I suppose you're right. I bet they never find the low-life responsible for this...they never do! I hate how our community lives under that ridiculous "snitch free code" even when it can bring closure to those in need." I stated.

"I hate to be a bitch...but you know what they say about karma. Her attack was clearly personal. You'd have to hate someone to do that to them. She royally pissed someone off and they retaliated." Cee Cee countered.

I agreed with Cee Cee and told her I needed to put Sincere to bed. I told her I loved her as always and promised I'd see her tomorrow. I had toyed with the idea of telling her about Noel but to be honest, I was a little embarrassed. I knew that she would ask me how he looked and I didn't have any answers for her. Besides, this was a one-time date. It would never ever happen again.

« Chapter 21 Thirsty »

The Past "Eli"

HAD IT NOT BEEN FOR the fact that I didn't want to leave any evidence behind, I would have spit on Trey's lifeless body. He had done a pretty good job at dodging me but as you can tell by his lack of oxygen...not quite good enough. Every time he crossed my mind I saw pure red. What would possess him to test my gangsta the way he had? What outcome was he expecting to derive from this?

I still couldn't look at Malia. She had broken my heart. I had put my little sister on a pedestal and was having a difficult time accepting that she was out there doing big girl things. I could tell that my silent treatment and disappointment was getting to her. She stayed in her room and cried a lot. Her attempts to apologize were quickly dismissed. I just couldn't forgive her right now.

All of her tests came back negative and she agreed to stop seeing Trey after being caught. She was hurt after discovering that he already had a family at home. Under normal circumstances the police would've been called and made aware of this illegal union, however this bullshit called for street justice. No one would rob me of the opportunity to snuff his life out.

It took me about a month to track him down but with the help of his baby momma, Pinky, I finally got his ass. Pinky and I used to fuck around back in the day. To be honest, she was the first bitch to ever throw a little pussy my way. That's probably one of the reasons why I never liked Trey's ass. She'd always be cool in my book.

Speaking of baby mommas', I was able to get my hands on some medications that induced abortions. The bottles that I read had the names Mifeprex and Cytotec on them...damn I cannot recall what the last bottle was. I had met this bad ass chick whose sister was a nurse at Planned Parenthood. I had managed to get her sister to hook me up...for a small fee of course. Operation Gia was next on my moderately long list.

∞

Approaching Gia's door, I watched as her front door swiftly swung open before I had the opportunity to knock. She was cheesing from ear to ear as she firmly embraced me. I hugged her back and pecked her on her cheek. Although her presence and happiness annoyed me, I was putting my charm into full gear.

Entering her apartment I was pleasantly surprised when I noticed she had baked chicken, rice pilaf and broccoli setting on the table. Now this shit was more like it. I had called her earlier telling her that we needed to talk about how we planned to coparent "our" baby.

What she didn't realize was there would be no baby. I was pretty certain that the baby wasn't mine, however I couldn't take any chances. No child of mine would ever come out of that hoe's pussy. I'd kill her first.

"Aye Gia, can you get me another cup of Kool-Aid? That shit is good as hell." I complimented scarfing down my meal.

I needed her to leave the room so that I could pour my concoction into her drink.

"Sure daddy, I got you." She smiled and grabbed my empty cup.

As soon as she disappeared into the kitchen I sprang into action.

I grabbed the prefilled syringe and squeezed its contents into her cup. I used her straw to give it a quick stir. I finished just in time as she quickly reentered the dining room.

"Here you go handsome."

"Thanks boo." I said with a phony smile.

Looking at her plate and glass of Kool-Aid, she had barely touched any of it. Growing concerned that she might not drink the concoction, I decided to try the romantic approach.

"Baby, you've barely touched anything. You need to feed my baby. Here let me feed you." I commanded, picking up her fork.

After giving her a couple of bites of her food, I decided it was time for her to wash it down. Handing her the glass, I watched anxiously as she downed the glass in two gulps and let out a huge belch.

"Thirsty?" I asked teasingly.

Appearing embarrassed she replied, "Excuse me. I'm sorry about that. I guess I was thirstier than I thought."

I smiled inwardly. I couldn't have cared less if the bitch had burped, farted and then shit on herself as long as she drank it.

"I'm surprised you liked this batch of Kool-Aid, it isn't as good as I typically make it. At least it was cold I guess." She shrugged.

"It was good to me boo. I have no complaints. Come over here, I have something warm for you to drink." I said while pulling my thick wood out.

I figured I would help the entire process along and fuck that fetus up out of her ass. I would kill her ass before I allowed anything containing half of my DNA to walk up out of her little twat.

∞

That concoction had taken a little longer than I'd anticipated. I was under the impression that they would take effect on the night I had her drink that Kool-Aid. I had started to panic a little and thought that my mission had failed until a devastated Gia texted me 911. I didn't want to be bothered with her, however, I decided to be the bigger person since I had a few hours to kill.

The emergency department had confirmed what we both already knew. There was nothing that anyone could do. She would have to wait for her body to expel the contents of her uterus naturally.

I held her for a couple of hours as she recanted how she had been hit with the strongest cramps of her life. She then experienced some heavy bleeding and knew then that she was miscarrying. On the inside I was doing the running man. I couldn't be happier! Of course, I had to console her and I told her that we'd make another one when the time was right.

What she failed to realize is I was never coming back. I knew that the bitch would try to trap me again if she ever caught me slipping. I was convinced that she wasn't suspicious regarding the cause of her miscarriage. Besides if she ever did in the future, there wouldn't be any way to prove it one way or the other. I stayed with her until she cried herself to sleep. I then walked out of her cramped apartment for good.

« Chapter 22 Smoking Gun »

The Past "Autumn"

A WISE MAN ONCE SAID, the quickest way to find a needle in the haystack is by burning that haystack. My sister, Wintress was that needle and between Don and I, no stone was left unturned. I had to give it to him, he worked tirelessly to find her. It had been about a month since we had received some promising leads, but now we had the smoking gun.

If it weren't for seeing her with my own two eyes, I probably wouldn't have believed that we had finally found her. Don had turned into a ruthless, cold-hearted killer. He had managed to track down several of the Price's relatives. Of course they all claimed to not know where the Price's and Wintress were hiding at.

I must say, they had some loyal people on their team...or maybe they truly did not know where they were. Unfortunately, none of that mattered to Don. He tortured and then killed them all the same. He stored their corpses in the same abandoned building.

One of Don's private investigators had received a tip that we should look into a house in East St. Louis. He was told that a little girl matching Wintress's description was seen coming and going from that specific location. We had been sent on so many wild goose chases that I truly didn't have much faith in this lead. However, I was a firm believer that every lead should be investigated.

Here I was looking at my little sister sitting on the front porch of a small rundown house. She looked so sad. It took everything in me to not just run up and snatch her up. We were supposed to be just casing the house out today and coming back tomorrow after we devised a plan. Seeing her now, I knew that I was not leaving without her. I didn't give a damn what Don had to say about it.

"Don, we have to get her today...now! Tomorrow may be too late. Look at her. She looks depressed. I'm not leaving without my sister. You can go if you want, but I'm not leaving her here!" I stated with finality.

Looking into my face and seeing my seriousness, Don simply shrugged his wide shoulders and said, "Okay."

I figured we'd just walk up to her and tell her to come with us and then leave. Of course, nothing was ever that easy right? As Don opened the gate leading to the house, Wintress looked up and her almond shaped eyes met mine. For a brief moment, I saw relief, but it was quickly replaced with fear.

She quickly stood up and ran screaming into the house. I heard her screaming, "Mom they're here! They are outside!!!"

"Who?!" I heard a woman ask.

"Autumn and that fat white man! They are outside!" She squealed.

In all of her excitement, she had failed to lock the door behind her. Don and I quickly gained access to the house and drew our weapons. In the foyer, Mrs. Price was seen standing behind Wintress while holding a silver gun to her head. The sight of this bitch holding a gun to my sister's head, drove me insane. She had crossed the line in so many ways that she had to die.

I was sick of blood being shed. I didn't want any more killings. I just simply wanted my sister back, but this bitch sealed her fate when she put that gun up to her head. One valuable lesson that I learned from Don is that you never draw your weapon unless you intend to use it.

All four of us initially participated in a stare down. We looked at on another with fear in our eyes. Don was the first one to speak up.

"Drop your weapon Tammy." He ordered.

"Fuck you! I'm not going to stand here and allow you two to kill me. You drop your weapons first!" She attempted to bargain.

"Mrs. Price, we have no intentions on killing you. I just want my sister back. It's all I've ever wanted. As soon as you let her go, we will leave and you will never hear from us again." I lied.

"Bullshit! After all me and my husband have done, you want us dead. I can't prove it, but I know you two are behind our family members disappearances. I can feel it in my bones!"

"Bitch! I said put the gun down! I'm hungry, hot and horny," he winked at me prior to continuing, "I have been chasing you guys down for too damn long. I've wasted a lot of time, money and resources behind your bullshit stunt. Give me my fucking daughter and we will be on our way!" With that his index finger appeared to tighten around the trigger.

I noticed Wintress throw a questioning glance his way but she remained silent.

"Why should I believe you assholes? You'd say any..." Before she could finish her sentence, I saw a huge hole tear into her forehead prior to her collapsing onto the ground and falling onto Wintress. My mouth flew open as I saw a stunned MaDonna still aiming at the exact spot Mrs. Price had stood only seconds before. Her gun was still smoking. She must've crept in through the back door.

MaDonna looked shocked. As much as I wanted to comfort her, I chose to comfort my sister instead. She was struggling to get from under Mrs. Price's dead weight. Flinging Mrs. Price off of my sister, I quickly embraced her in my arms. Feeling her in my arms and inhaling her familiar scent had me sobbing like a baby.

"Oh I've missed you so much Wintress!" I cried.

"Autumn, please don't be mad at me for running from you. Mom and dad...I mean the Price's told me that if I ever saw you again, that I better run. They told me that you hated me and wanted to kill me. They said you blamed me for mom dying. I can't believe that I listened to them. They told me that you were crazy now." She cried.

It broke my heart listening to the crazy things they'd attempted to brainwash her with. Gently lifting her chin up so that she could see the sincerity in my eyes I said, "You're my sister and I will always love you no matter what. Nothing or no one will ever change that. I'd never hurt you, not even on my craziest day."

With that we both chuckled.

The sound of a car door closing snapped us back into the seriousness of our situation. We had to get the hell out of that house. MaDonna was still frozen in place as Don picked her up and we took off towards the back door. Circling around the house and in the direction of the car, Mr. Price could be seen walking through the front door. His animalistic cries of grief could be heard as we peeled off, headed back over into Missouri territory.

∞

The months that followed were joyous ones for the most part. Both Wintress and I were performing well in school. She got along well with the boys as I knew she would. Mrs. Douglas was still grieving for her sister, but she still managed to find time for us kids. She welcomed Wintress into her home with open arms. We were almost one big happy family...with the exception of Don's obsession with me.

Of course now that he had held his end of the bargain and was able to find my sister, he took my body whenever he wanted it. At first, I felt this deep sense of obligation to him. I felt as if I owed him for reuniting us, however, at some point I started feeling as if my debt was paid already. I was sick of being his sex slave. He still disgusted me and made my skin crawl. When no one was around, he'd call me Celeste. Whenever I tried to deny him, he would always threaten to send me to another foster home.

Thoughts of losing my sister again always made me put my big girl panties on and suffer through Don's bullshit. By this time, I was completely and madly in love with MaDonna. She was like a breath of fresh air. She gave me the complete opposite feeling that Don did. We were inseparable for the most part throughout the day. Don rarely allowed sleepovers because that was when he wanted me all for himself.

After much coaxing, I had finally confessed to MaDonna about me and Don's strange relationship. She wanted to kill him of course. As much as I would've loved to permanently erase him from my life, I knew that for now he was a temporary fixture. He was the one who held the power as to whether or not I saw Wintress. He was her biological father, while I was just a high school student. I'd never be granted custody.

I had come to realize that even after I turned eighteen, he

would not give me custody of her. I would essentially be powerless until Wintress turned eighteen and was able to legally make her own decisions. I'd never leave her with him. I shuddered at the thought of having to stomach him for that long. I couldn't risk losing her again, not even for my love for MaDonna.

« Chapter 23 It's Complicated »

The Past "Gladys"

TO SAY THAT THE RELATIONSHIP between Omar and I was confusing, would be an understatement. While I stood firm on us not getting back together, I felt him latching himself onto me. He had practically moved in with me, but he slept in a different room. He'd even taken the semester off to help me around the house. Despite him getting on my nerves and smothering me, I guess you can say that he and I had become good friends.

I had become spoiled and relied heavily on him to help me out. I was now just a couple of weeks away from my due date and was now on bedrest. Omar had really stepped up to the plate. It was almost hard to remember that he had abandoned us for the first months of my pregnancy. He still worked during the day, but would frequently check on me throughout the day. I had given him access to my accounts and he was making sure that my household bills were paid.

My days were spent reading textbooks, watching tv and stuffing my face with unhealthy fried foods. My professors were allowing me to complete my studies from home. I was so blessed that Omar was self-less enough to put his future career on hold to care for me and our unborn child.

Two days prior to my due date, I was restless and ready to drop my load. I was officially sick of lying around the house. I needed some fresh air! Omar wasn't home so I decided to take a walk around my neighborhood. Omar was running unusually late and we weren't fortunate enough to have cellphones back then. I quickly scribbled 'I went for a walk' on a notepad and left.

My obstetrician had told me that walking helped to induce labor. I prayed that was true. I felt as if I had been pregnant for years! The sun felt amazing on my skin. The warm air was refreshing and smelled so clean. It was refreshing seeing the neighborhood children playing as the elderly people sat nosily on their porches. As I continued to waddle down the street, I realized that I'd forgotten to grab my water bottle. It was a fairly warm evening and my mouth was dry.

Instead of going back home, I decided to stop by a nearby convenience store and pick up a bottle of water. I rejoiced inwardly as Sam's Mini Mart drew near. Breathing heavily, I could almost taste the cold water going down my parched throat. As I reached for the door, it was pushed open by none other than Lukas's sexy ass.

He was still by far the sexiest man that I had ever seen in my life. He looked as if he had stepped directly out of a GQ magazine. I licked my lips as we both stood staring into each other's eyes. Oh, how I missed that man. I'd forgotten all about...what was his name??? Oh yes, Omar! I had almost forgotten about...oh no! Our baby!

I think our thoughts and our eyes fell on my protruding belly at the same time. Lukas's eyes were the size of saucers and his mouth would certainly be catching flies soon. I felt so incredibly exposed and ashamed. How could I have done this to Lukas? He had asked me to wait for him. I occasionally glanced at Lukas and his eyes had yet to leave my stomach. He looked so bewildered and disappointed.

Neither of us apparently knew what to say. I grew tired of the awkward stare down and turned on my heels and attempted to run my big pregnant behind back the way I had come from. I swiftly felt someone embrace me into a firm bear hug from behind. Being in Lukas's arms felt so great and it made me realize even more how much I truly missed him.

Still standing on the sidewalk with his arms around me, his hands travelled down to my belly and I felt his hot tears flowing down my neck. I felt so bad.

"Why didn't you tell me G? I would've been there for the both of you. Come move in with me. I'll take care of you and her." He whispered so softly that I barely heard him.

"I'm so sorry Lukas. I should've waited for you but some of the things your revealed about yourself truly left me devastated. It broke my heart. I missed you so much. You were the best friend that I ever had, aside from my dad. How do you know it's a girl?" I asked.

"I just know she is a girl and she will be as beautiful as you are. I've changed a lot G. I'm not into those same illegal activities anymore. Hey guess what?"

"What?"

"I'm in college now majoring in business. I'm the proud owner of a laundromat too. Business has been good. I've turned my dirty money into clean money G." He boasted.

Turning around to face him, I smiled brightly. "I'm so proud of you! I knew you could do it Lukas! The sky is the limit for you!" I squealed and pecked him on his cheek.

I was genuinely happy for him. This was the best news that I'd received in a while.

"I guess I should be getting back. Omar will be worried about me. It was so nice seeing you. Let's keep in touch. Okay?" I stated.

He looked annoyed for a moment before stating, "Most definitely G. The least I can do is drop you off and I will not take no for an answer. Come on." He said not allowing me time to object.

Approaching my house, I noticed two cars parked in my driveway. I signaled for Lukas to slow down. Omar was seen getting out of his vehicle and walking over to the driver's side of the other vehicle. The driver appeared to be a young white woman. Omar bent down and tongued the floozie down in front of my house. I couldn't believe that he had the gull to be so disrespectful. Technically, we weren't together, but I assumed that we were working towards something.

I didn't even realize that I was crying until I felt Lukas hand me some Kleenexes. I felt humiliated. If I never saw him again, it would be too soon! When he passed my house, I didn't even object. I wasn't in the mood to argue with Omar right now. I sat quietly in the passenger side of Lukas's car wondering where we were headed. I could've told him to take me to the dorm room that I still shared with Paige, however. I stared ahead while he rubbed my belly.

He drove for about ten minutes until we pulled up to a beautiful house in Hazelwood. It was just the perfect size. The yard was well-manicured and large. As we entered the house, Lukas deactivated his security system. What I truly loved about the house was that it felt homey.

"Come in and make yourself comfortable Gladys. I'll whip us up some bacon cheese burgers and fries...just the way you like it." Lukas replied with a gorgeous smirk.

I simply smiled and nodded before replying, "Don't forget my vanilla shake...extra thick."

While Lukas was preoccupied with making our meal, I took it upon myself to explore his home. The house was bigger than my own, but it was no mansion. It was beautifully decorated and very clean. I counted four bedrooms and three bathrooms. I claimed a room down the hall from what I assumed was the master bedroom. I had no idea how long I would take refuge here, I only knew that I had no desire to face Omar right now.

I was finally able to see where Lukas laid his head. He was always so secretive and never revealed much about himself. We'd crossed a major milestone in our friendship today. I knew with me being so close to my due date that I'd have to face Omar sooner than later. Our living arrangement as we knew it was definitely not going to work out once our child arrived.

I didn't want my child confused and to think that it was okay to shack up with a man, even if it were their father. Yes, a change was certainly about to come.

« Chapter 24 My Family »

The Past "Lukas"

SEEING GLADYS AFTER SO much time was a pleasant surprise. However, seeing a pregnant Gladys was like a slap in the face. I'll be the first to admit that seeing her pregnant brought about many emotions that most men would be ashamed to acknowledge they possess. I wanted to hug her, kiss her, protect her. I also wanted to scream at her, slap her and force her to get rid of *that* baby.

I'd longed for her for her so long, but the possibility of her being pregnant by someone else never crossed my mind. I knew that I had to accept her baby as mine from this day forward. I knew she'd expect nothing less of me. While she looked beautiful as usual in front of Sam's Mini Mart, I knew she wasn't truly happy. Her lame as boyfriend was now breathing on borrowed time. I'd never allow another man to continue living after being inside of Gladys. I was supposed to be her first, her only. She failed to wait on me and that hurt.

I knew the positive changes that I'd made in my life were necessary; however, it made me feel some type of way. It made me feel as if nothing I'd ever do would be good enough for her. Watching her practically getting cheated on in front of *her* house just further confirmed that her lame ass little boyfriend had to go. He'd never raise the baby that I had already claimed as my own.

A day after G arrived at my house, she confronted Omar over the phone. She told him that she wanted him out of her house before their baby was born. The possessive side of me wanted to interrupt her ass and tell her that it wasn't that fool's baby. I remained silent and allowed her to speak for herself. When asked how Omar took the news, she stated that he was upset but agreed to leave her house that day.

A week went by and we were closer than ever. I don't know why, but I had an overwhelming feeling to make an honest woman out of her. I went out and purchased a 14k white gold ring with a pink heart shaped 4k diamond. Naturally, the band itself was encrusted with diamonds as well. I decided to propose to her one evening while we watched 'Imitation of Life'. That girl loved that movie!

"Hey G, you know I adore the hell out of you right?" I reminded her.

"You better adore me big head." She teased in response.

"Being around you again like this has made me realize that I never want to be without you in my life ever again." I stated dropping down onto one knee in front of her.

I continued, "Would you please do me the honor of being my wife? I already love the little girl that you are carrying as my own. I want to give you both my last name...right now. Tonight!" I confessed, while showcasing the beautiful ring I'd purchased just for this occasion.

"Wow, Lukas. I was not expecting this...it's a lot to think about..." She started.

"Don't think about it baby. Let's go and do this. I'll always protect you. Cherish you. I will never step out on you or our marriage. I promise." I bellowed. I personally thought I sounded pretty damn convincing. For an added effect, I allowed a lone tear to trickle down my face as I showcased my most irresistible smile.

"I love you girl. Besides, I know this is what your father would have wanted..." I made sure to lay it on extra thick.

She appeared to be in deep thought as she rubbed on her oversized midsection. After what seemed like an eternity she squealed, "Let's do this Mr. Monroe! Put my ring on!!!"

I happily obliged and gave her the biggest kiss on the lips. I don't why, but I just had to have this woman.

∞

I knew with Gladys being ready to drop her load any day now, we couldn't stray too far. I was pretty sure that G would be more than happy to marry me so I had rented out a small hall. I had invited the few people that we each carried near and dear to our hearts. I knew that the dress that I'd picked out for Gladys probably wouldn't be the greatest fit, but hell I tried. I looked damn good in my tux, if I must say so myself.

It was nice to see G laughing and truly enjoying herself. Her friend Paige helped out a lot. What G didn't know was that Paige was on my payroll as well. She was one of my top hoes. That broad made me a lot of money!

After the ceremony, I escorted my beautiful new bride to the honeymoon suite that I planned for us to stay in until she went into labor.

There was something about marriage that made your partner so much more beautiful. G had a certain glow to her. She had more than just the usual pregnancy glow. She was beyond beautiful to me. I couldn't believe that we had made everything official. I had done a lot of crazy shit in my life, however, this superseded them all by far!

As she freshened up in the bathroom, I thought about how close I was to finally fucking Gladys. I had daydreamed about her numerous times, but I was beginning to think that I'd never see it come to fruition. After approximately twenty minutes, my wife stepped out of the bathroom in nothing, but her ebony skin and her five-inch red heels. She was the epitome of a beautiful black goddess.

As she walked slowly over to the bed, I couldn't help but to think about how one of the biggest forms of disrespect to another man was to fuck the woman who carried their child. Under normal circumstances, I'd never fuck a pregnant woman that wasn't pregnant with my child. It was an unspoken code. However, this was now my bitch and my child. I was about to place all types of dents into the baby's scalp.

G stopped right in front of me. I was like a kid in a toy store and didn't know what I wanted to play with first. I had so many options. Since her left breast was within a tongue's reach of my mouth, I engulfed damn near her entire titty. My right hand went to work tweaking her right nipple while my left played with the pearl between her legs.

She moaned so seductively. I glanced up at her and noticed that her head had rolled back. I felt her knees buckle as she coated my left hand with her sweet juices. Not wanting any part of my new wife to go to waste, I hungrily licked the juices from each of my fingers.

Laying her onto her back, I spread her legs as far as she allowed me to. She was so wet that two of my fingers slide inside of her with ease. I loved the way her tight walls threatened to cut off the circulation in my fingers. I was determined to make her cum at least ten times before I even thought about pleasing myself.

I could tell that her lame ass ex wasn't pleasing her right.

She was starving for the attention, love and foreplay that she was receiving. Hooking my fingers in an upward position, I watched G become possessed with euphoric ecstasy. She attempted to push me away a few times, but I wouldn't allow it.

By this time she was howling and lifting her plump ass off the bed.

"Oh Lukas! Oh my goodness Lukas! I'm cumming!!! Unnnhhhhhh!" She shrieked as I attempted to catch all of her in my mouth.

Of course, it proved to be a difficult feat. Her essence found its way dribbling down my chin, neck and onto my chest. That was some of the sexiest shit I'd ever been involved in. She tasted so sweet. I wondered if the pregnancy made her this sweet or if she always tasted that way.

I dove head first into her moist center. She almost immediately clamped her legs tightly around my head.

"Lukas! I can't take anymore babbbbbbbby! No more pleaaaasssssseeee!!!" She begged with tears rolling out of the corners of her gorgeous eyes.

I looked up at her smugly and asked her if she was ready to feel me inside of her and she quickly nodded her head.

I wiped my mouth and decided to tease her a little bit. I removed all of my clothes and laid on top of her being careful not to put any of my weight on her belly. I then took my engorged dick and rubbed it up and down her slit. I intentionally bypassed her hole and occasionally tapped my member against her throbbing clit. I could feel her thrusting upward in an attempt to get my dick to slide inside of her.

Suddenly she screamed, "Luke! Get up! I think my fucking water just broke!!!"

I knew shit was real because I'd never heard G curse before. Glancing down, I noticed that there was an unusual amount of fluids on the bed.

"I think I'm going into labor Luke!" She yelled as I pulled away and noticed that she'd released the Niagara Falls from between her legs.

"Oh shit, what did I do?! Is it my fault?!" I stupidly asked in my panic.

"I don't know...maybe. My obstetrician told me that sexual activity can induce labor. Please get me to a hospital! This shit hurts baby!" She writhed in pain.

"Oh yeah, please don't forget to call Omar. Although I'm upset with him, I don't want him to miss our child being born!" She blurted out in agony.

Getting dressed, I devilishly nodded. This bitch had me all the way fucked up if she thought this nigga would ever see my daughter!

« Chapter 25 Moving On »

The Past "Mike"

OCTOBER THIRD IS A DAY that I'll never ever forget. Here I was just a couple of months into my college experience when I was blindsided by the most horrific news imaginable. I was at football practice confidently running back and forth on *my* field. I was most certainly destined for greatness even if I had to say so myself. We had a very strong team, however I was clearly the star.

Just as I was about to tackle one of my opponents, I stopped dead in my tracks. Rushing down the bleachers was a man who looked just like my grandfather. The same one I'd previously lied and told Alicia had died when we first started seeing each other. As he continued to descend down the steps, I knew it was definitely my old man.

Why on Earth would he be here? A feeling of dread automatically washed over me because of how panicked he looked and how fast he was attempting to get to me. Coming out of my daze, I decided to meet him half way. Forgetting that I was in the middle of practice, I took off in his direction.

Upon reaching the bleachers, I took two steps at a time. As fast as I was on the field, I felt as if I were moving in slow motion. After what felt like an eternity, I finally reached my old man.

"Hey pops, what are you doing here? What's wrong?" I asked quickly on the verge of losing my mind.

I braced myself for the verbal blow that I knew was inevitably coming.

"Sit down son." He commanded.

As exhausted as I was from practice, my adrenaline now prevented me from wanting to sit.

"I'm okay pops, please tell me what is going on!" I pleaded.

"I said, sit...down!" His voice boomed. My grandfather had a powerful voice, similar to that of James Earl Jones.

I finally did as I was told. I stared at him waiting for him to tell me what all of this was about.

"Michael, I'm not gonna bullshit you son. Someone has killed your momma. Lord, my daughter is gone!" He wailed as he collapsed to his knees.

This was the saddest shit that I had ever witnessed or been a part of. I had never seen my grandfather cry. He was a strong, proud man. Sadly he looked so fragile and broken in that moment.

I hadn't quite processed the words that he had just spoken. I was too focused on the man who I've always looked up to, falling apart before my very eyes.

Once I was able to digest what he'd actually said and what the reason behind his misery was, I went ape shit.

"Yo pops, what do you fucking mean someone killed my momma?! That shit can't be real. I just saw her yesterday. She cannot be dead. This shit is a mistake. How do they know it's her?!" I rambled in utter devastation.

Typically my grandfather would have caved my chest in for speaking to him that way, but I wasn't even sure he had heard me through his own grief. I sat down in stunned silence, unsure of how to console my pops. The men in our family never showed much emotion or affection towards one another so I just waited it out.

No one cried forever...right?

After a while, he composed himself enough to speak.

"Mike, the police showed up at my house this morning. They informed me that your mother was out walking her dog when she was robbed and shot twice in the head by her attacker(S). She died instantly. They had me come down to the medical examiner's office to identify her. I can't believe they did that to my baby!" He recounted before breaking down again.

My heart sank knowing how my mother's final moments ended. She spent her last few minutes in fear. My mother was the most generous and caring person and would've happily given those bastards anything they asked for. Killing her was completely unnecessary.

Lost in my thoughts I heard my old man wail, "They even shot her fucking dog Michael! You know how much she loved that damn dog!" He sobbed.

Hearing this I buried my face into my fists and broke down. What kind of monsters would do such a thing?! How would I go on without her? Someone not only robbed me of the most important person in my life, but they robbed my kids too. My kids would never know the amazing person their grandmother was.

After those thoughts penetrated my mind, I lost it. I remember yelling uncontrollably as I begin banging my head on the bleachers. I vaguely recall my old man attempting to stop me but his efforts were rendered useless against my strength. In between my self-inflicted blows, I could hear my teammates rushing towards me.

"Who killed my fucking momma???!!!" Is the last thing I recall before the last blow shrouded me in total darkness.

∞

Okay, so I lied...sue me! It had been three weeks and I still hadn't killed Shay or Tamar. Shay was a damn cash cow. She had an ATM between her battered thighs. Her body count over the past few weeks had surpassed a couple of hundred. A couple of hundred guys at five-hundred a head...you do the math! It didn't take a genius to figure out why I had spared the bitch for so long. My mom's unexpected death also had me feeling a little more compassionate lately.

At this point, I didn't keep either of them tied up. Shay was usually too weak and tired to try to escape and Tamar knew I'd fuck her nubby hand ass up if she tried any funny business with me. She actually helped me a lot with keeping Shay up. The niggas that came by definitely wouldn't be shelling out five-hundred dollars for an unkempt bitch.

Shay always looked like a dime piece just before my niggas ravaged her every day. The birth control that she was on made her periods nonexistent and I was truly grateful for this. I didn't want to miss out on that type of money for something as insignificant as a bloody pussy.

It was tough balancing everything. I was raking in enough money to pay one of my homies, Playboy, to watch the women while I was at school, at football practice or a game, seeing my son and boosting the latest gear. Of course, my homie could also use Shay as an added incentive. With my mom gone, I had decided to bring my daughter Michaela to the warehouse to be with Shay. It made the breastfeeding process much easier.

Shay's mom had called twice asking if I had seen either Shay or Michaela and I told the bitch no. She told me that she was going to go downtown to file a missing person's report. I told her to let me know if there was anything that I could do to help.

When the news broke of Sha'Keisha's death, I couldn't have been happier. I knew that I hadn't left any witnesses behind. I was afraid of her regaining consciousness and ratting me out to the authorities.

School was going well. I was surprisingly acing all of my freshman classes. I knew how important it was that I maintained a decent G.P.A. My scholarship depended on it. My team had yet to lose a game. We were definitely experiencing a winning streak. Nobody could touch us! We were simply the best.

Losing my mom had thrown me for a loop. I had a rough few days, but I then came back swinging harder than I ever had before in my life. My mom was greatly loved and missed within our community. The news covered her death nonstop. Everyone was outraged by the brutality and randomness of this attack. It could've happened to anyone and that was the most frightening part of it all. People were forced to face their own mortality.

Over a thousand mourners came to pay their respects to my mother. Through her work as a child advocate, she knew everyone. My mother didn't have a single enemy in this world. At her funeral I just sat there in a trance. I do not remember much, nor do I want to.

I sulked for a few days, but on day four, I told myself that life must go on. I had kids who depended on me. Despite my coach's advice to sit out for a few games, I refused. Sitting around with too much idle time only made things worse. Luckily he didn't put up too much of a fight because he knew he needed me. They were nothing without me.

Now my relationship with Alicia is still not all that great. I had lied to her a couple of weeks ago and told her that I had taken care of Tamar and Shay. I guess it wasn't exactly a lie...I did take care of them both in one way or the other. It took some convincing, but she does believe that they are both dead now. The thing that pisses me off is the fact that it doesn't seem as if it has made a difference. She is still short with me.

If it isn't about Sincere then she isn't interested in talking to me. She's different. I can't quite put my finger on it, but Alicia is very different from the way she used to be. I want my baby back. I fucking hate that free will bullshit. I wish that I could control her thoughts, emotions and her heart. I'd make her love me the way she used to. I'm not a bad dude. I was good to her ass. Sure, we had some problems along the way, but what relationship hasn't?

One Saturday evening, I decided to stop by to see Alicia and Sincere. I had been begging her to move in with me, but she wanted no parts in that conversation. Ringing her doorbell, I waited a couple of minutes. I could hear movement coming from inside her house, but figured she was ignoring me like she does occasionally. Finally Alicia opened the door with only a towel covering her body and one on her head. She appeared surprised and disappointed to see me.

I instantly rocked up and licked my lips at the sight and scent of her. She had opened the door looking like a straight snack. I didn't know if she knew it or not, but I wasn't leaving without getting some pussy. Picking her up, I was glad when she didn't resist. I slammed and locked the front door with my free hand. I brought my princess into her room and gently laid her onto her stomach.

"Get on your knees." I ordered.

She did as asked without a word.

I walked up behind her and dove head first into her asshole. My tongue expertly flicked back and forth as I watched her claw at the sheets underneath us. Knowing what drove her over the top I trailed my tongue towards her soaked box and then again towards her ass.

Her moans ranged from her calling out for Jesus and then for me. She came in my mouth three times before I showed her any mercy. I wanted to show her everything that she'd been missing. I prayed that she'd finally lighten up with me and take me back. I missed everything about her red ass.

Coming up for air, I positioned myself behind her, prepared to enter her from behind. She swiftly ordered me to stop and rolled out of position.

"Look Mike, I appreciate you stopping by, because I've been worried about you...but this was a mistake. I feel so bad about your mom and I know you are hurting. Having sex will not mend your broken heart. I'm sorry to have led you on, but I'm not fucking you. You should leave." She demanded looking at the clock on her nightstand.

Feeling down, but prepared to respect her wishes, I asked to see my son before I left.

"Cee Cee is babysitting Sincere for me tonight because I..." She trailed.

Studying her face, she looked both guilty and fearful.

"You what Alicia? It looks like you're going out. Who are you going out with tonight? It must be important if you have muthafuckas babysitting my son. Where the fuck are you headed to and with who?!" I yelled.

Attempting to appear brave, she replied, "Mike please leave. What I am doing and who I am doing it with no longer concerns you. I am single and I've moved on. Again I suggest you do the same.

Before she could finish her last sentence I felt myself rush her ass. I ran into her with so much force that she flew back onto the hardwood floor with a thud. She was out cold. This bitch must have thought that I was playing when I told her that she'd die before I allowed her to be with the next nigga.

Deciding that now was as good a time as any to get my nut off, I climbed on top of my unconscious baby momma and roughly entered her. I swear, every time I fucked her, the pussy got better and better. I moaned and talked dirty to her ass as if she could hear me.

It was different pummeling her limp body. A little moaning and back scratching on her behalf would've been nice. Deciding that the cold hard floor was hurting my knees, I decided to finally nut. I bit my lip to keep from yelling out in ecstasy. I loved her so fucking much. I emptied my seeds into her warm opening and caught my breath as I tried to think of what to do next.

Picking her up, I brought her into her bathroom. Putting the stopper into the drain, I began to fill her tub up with warm water. I begin to cry as I laid my beautiful Queen into the tub.

"It didn't have to end like this Alicia. I gave you a part of me that no other woman can ever say she possessed...my heart. I would've done anything for you." I said roughly kissing her lips.

I watched as the tub slowly filled up, yet she seemed to float on top. Just as I was about to push her head under the water, I heard the front door open as her mother and sisters walked in. Snapping back into reality, I quickly jumped up. I turned the water off, pulled the stopper out and escaped through her bedroom window as I had numerous times in the past. Reaching my car, I noticed a baby blue BMW pull up to my girl's house.

Too curious to care about escaping, I sat back and watched as an ugly ass ape-like nigga got out of the car and walked up to her front door. Who the fuck and what the fuck was he doing there? She couldn't seriously have considered replacing me with that muthafucka. His appearance was insult to a sexy nigga like me.

He stood on the porch for a few moments before Alicia's panic-stricken mother opened the door and allowed him to enter. She must have located Alicia which meant the law would be coming soon. I slowly pulled off praying that Alicia wouldn't snitch me out. She should be thankful that I had allowed her to live.

As I drove past the Ape's car, I wrote down his license plate number. I didn't know who or even what the hell he was, but one thing was clear...he was dead meat. Alicia was my bitch!

« Chapter 26 Just A Dream »

The Past "Celeste"

AFTER SHAWN DROPPED ME off at my car the morning after we'd made love for the very first time, I couldn't help but be embarrassed. He had refused to talk to me throughout the rest of the night or during the drive to pick up my car from my school. Before getting out of his car, I glanced at him and asked one final time what I had done wrong. I had personally enjoyed the sex and was pretty sure that he had as well until we were finished.

His demeanor had changed almost instantaneously. His final words to me the night before still stung like a bee. I had known Shawn my entire life and never thought he'd treat me this way. He was my best friend besides Alicia, how could he say those things to me. To me?!

I had given myself to him and now he was acting like a complete dickhead. I couldn't for the life of me think of why he'd think I wasn't a virgin. I was a virgin. Eli and I had fooled around a few times, but he had never penetrated me. I had never been around any other guy, so I was at a loss. I needed answers, however, I knew that Shawn would not be offering up any, any time soon.

Looking at the expression on his face, I knew my presence disgusted him. That broke my heart because I could always count on his great big dimpled smile to bring me comfort. Shawn was always so supportive and thoughtful. I didn't recognize the stranger sitting beside me.

"Shawn, I am not sure what I've done to you or if I've offended you in anyway. I apologize from the bottom of my heart for whatever it is. Can you please just talk to me please?! I haven't slept with anyone else but you. I would've told you Shawn, I promise. Please..." I begged.

The bastard never even blinked. I saw him starting to work his jaw and decided that I better leave him alone. I'd seen him get into fights with guys before and he'd always work his jaw beforehand. I was no fool. Heartbroken, I quickly slid out of the passenger side of his car. Before I could close the door good, he sped off leaving me standing there looking crazy.

I instantly broke down crying. What the fuck was wrong with him?! Did my coochie stink or something? What did I do?! Sadly walking to my car, I cried for what seemed like an eternity once I got inside. I was jonsing for my pain medicine but my vision was blurred by my tears. I couldn't safely drive until I calmed down a little.

After I was all cried out, I attempted to compose myself. I grabbed a pack of baby wipes out of my glove compartment and wiped the tears and snot from my face. I then applied some lotion and put on some sunglasses. My eyes were now swollen and sensitive to the bright sun. Finally pulling out my school parking lot, I turned in the direction of the closest Walgreens.

I wasn't in the mood to get out or bump into someone I knew, so I simply drove up to the drive-thru window to fill my script.

After verifying my address and handing my prescription over, I watched the young pharmacy tech read over my patient profile for a few moments.

"Ms. Monroe, it is too soon to fill your script. Let me see when you can fill it again okay?" The pharmacy tech finally stated.

"That will be great, thanks." I said getting nervous.

I needed my medicine and I needed it now! I had already exceeded my threshold fucking around with Shawn. What was I going to do?! My mind raced fast as hell as I thought about people who I might be able to buy the pills from on the street. I had plenty of money saved up so it shouldn't be a problem. I would definitely have to be more cautious when I filled my pills next time. I went through them way too fast.

"Ma'am, it looks as if you have about three weeks left until you can fill this prescription which will be the 27th. Did you consume that entire bottle already?" The nosy pharmacy tech inquired, interrupting me from my thoughts.

"No, I lost my bottle and I'm in a great deal of pain. Is there anything that can be done? I can't wait three weeks before receiving my pain medication. I was in a terrible accident and broke several bones in my body. Please help me out ma'am." I pleaded. The thought of having to wait weeks for my medicine scared me to death.

"Unfortunately, you will have to contact your PCP. If by chance he buys your bullshit story, he may write you another script. In the meantime, I suggest you get some help." She replied handing me a drug abuse flyer.

"Fuck you!" Is all I managed to yell out as I sped off. Was it that obvious that my pain medications were becoming a little problem. Well, they were really a very small problem. I could stop whenever I wanted to. Right now, I needed them to numb my pain. I'd stop soon.

∞

I had been driving around for two hours without luck. I

couldn't find anyone who was selling the pills that I was seeking. They were all selling hardcore shit that I wasn't interested in. I was running out of time and needed to head home so that I could shower and prepare for work. I hated to go into work feeling this way but I also hated calling in. I had just returned after being hospitalized for months. I didn't want to push my luck.

Upon entering my house, I saw my mom at the kitchen table grading her students' papers. Thankfully she was so focused that she barely noticed me as I came in. I quickly greeted her, pecked her on her cheek and darted upstairs. I was cutting it close so I took a super quick shower and was on my way to Divas R Us.

Typically I absolutely loved my job and looked forward to coming, but not today. My shift could not end fast enough. Every question a customer asked struck a nerve. I was sweating, sore and ready to explode. I couldn't stay still. I needed my damn medicine!

"Hey Celeste, can I see you in my office please?" Joe requested.

"Sure, I'll be there in a second." I responded.

Once I finished hanging up the remaining dresses, I headed back to Joe's office. It had been a while since I'd ventured off in there, but there I stood.

"Joe, you wanted to see me?" I asked anxiously. All I could focus on was getting this monkey off my back. My skin was crawling by this point. I would surely flunk out of school if I had to sit through class feeling like this on Monday.

"Yes, close the door and have a seat." He instructed.

I did as I was told. It took everything in me not to fidget around.

"Celeste the reason why I brought you in here is because I've received several complaints from both the customers as well as your coworkers. They are reporting erratic, hostile behaviors. Now I've known you long enough to know that these behaviors are out of character for you. I've been hearing that you've been overusing your prescription pain medication.

Now I could drug test you, but I already know that it will come back positive for the medication that you have a prescription for. There is no harm in taking the medication as prescribed but you are overdoing it. I'm not going to fire you, although I know I probably should. I've never had any problems with your work performance before and we are not about to start now. You will not come to my place of business like this ever again. Next time you will not be so lucky.

Lucky for you, I have encountered a pill head or two in my day. I know the antidote for your problem is a little Lorazepam. I have plenty to spare. I'm supposed to take that shit every day to help my nerves and stress but I don't. It makes me sleepy and slows me down when I need to be most alert. Here take a couple of these and lay down on that couch over there. I'll take you home later."

I happily threw two of the pills down my throat. I later found out that they were one milligram each. I didn't even bother reading the bottle. I just needed to be relieved of my misery. Joe walked with me over to the couch. He removed my shoes and laid a warm quilt over me.

Within thirty minutes, I was off to a fitful sleep. I was having those crazy dreams again and they felt so real. I dreamt that Joe had removed my pants and panties and was having sex with me. It felt so real. I could see him, feel him, hear him and smell him. I could feel him lightly nibbling on my nipples and occasionally rubbing on my clit.

In my dream he was a much better lover than Shawn. Each stroke was fragmented as if the lights were being flickered off and on. I had died and gone to heaven when he went downtown. When he came up from eating me out, I hungrily accepted his tongue into my mouth and happily tasted my own juices.

"I love you Celeste. I fucking love you! I will leave her, all you have to do is ask." I heard him moan over and over again as if trying burn his words into my soul.

I do not recall anything else about that dream. I just remember Joe waking me up hours later telling me that it was time to go home. Remembering that wild dream, I glanced down and saw no evidence that we had had sex. My clothes were intact and he seemed to be acting like his normal self.

"Joe I really appreciate everything that you do for me and for not firing me today. I do love my job here. I promise I will never behave that way again." I assured him.

"No need to thank me Celeste. You have blessed me more than you'll ever know. You are my best worker and I'd hate to lose you over nonsense. As far as I'm concerned, you will always have a job here."

"That is such a huge relief. I hate to ask, but do you think that I can have some of that Lorenzo-pam...or whatever you called it?" I laughed nervously.

"Of course, I told you before there's nothing I wouldn't do for you. Here are a couple of bottles. Only take 1-2 when you feel you really need it. Try not to take it before school or before driving. It makes you extremely drowsy...especially in the beginning. Try not to get too carried away with this because it can also be very addictive. Do you understand me?"

I nodded my head quickly as I took the bottles from him.

"Can I get a hug?" He asked.

"Sure Joe, thanks again for understanding." I stated sincerely.

He wrapped his strong arms around me and I couldn't help but think about how familiar he felt and smelled in my arms. I'd even noticed the soreness in my pussy for the first time since I had awakened. Maybe my period was coming. As he embraced me, I pushed him away as I felt his wood stiffening up and poking me in my abdomen.

Why did this shit seem like deja vu? It was all just a dream wasn't it?!

« Chapter 27 Then There Were Two»

The Past "Gladys"

MARRIED LIFE WITH LUKAS was so good in the beginning. I was in awe of the beautiful bouncing baby girl who I lovingly named Celeste as promised. Thankfully Paige was in town and was able to be there for Celeste's birth. I was in labor for a mere fifty-eight minutes before my precious impatient baby entered the world.

I think seeing Celeste had triggered certain memories and she had revealed that she had a two year old son named Shawn. Her mother had decided to take care of Shawn while she attended college. I was stunned. Why had she never told me about her kid before? I never kept any secrets from my bestie. I told her that I wanted to meet him as soon as possible. I wanted our kids to know each other and be best friends.

After much consideration, we decided that Lukas would be listed as the father on Celeste's birth certificate. We were unable to reach Omar to inform him that I was in labor. He missed everything, so Lukas manned up and filled his shoes.

When people reveal themselves to you, take heed and steer clear of them. I shouldn't have allowed Omar to come back into my life after he abandoned me during the beginning of my pregnancy. I guess the maternal side of me wanted to do everything in my power to make us work.

I then had to witness the father of my child practically cheating on me in front of my home in broad daylight. I stayed away for a few weeks prior to returning home. Now that I was married, I had decided to move in with my husband.

I dreaded going to my own home because I didn't want to run into Omar. I wasn't ready to discuss the rock on my ring finger or the fact that I had named his daughter after another man. However, I needed clothes, toiletries and my textbooks. I also needed to pick up things for Celeste. I just didn't want to face him. I couldn't face him. I wanted to avoid the conflict. I prayed that he'd gotten the hint and would be long gone when I returned.

I suppose my prayers were answered...in a way. Yes, he was gone, but so was practically everything of value in my home. The TVs, the stereo system, appliances, item's I'd purchased for my daughter, even my dad's beloved baseball card collection.

The bastard even had the audacity to leave me a note on a wrinkled piece of paper that simply read, 'Sorry, but I needed it more than you. I will pay you back as soon as I can. Kiss my baby for me. Love O.'

I was so hurt and in such a state of disbelief that I couldn't even cry. I glanced around my bare living room seeing only red. I was on the verge of seriously snapping and I had to pray for God to calm me down. The thoughts that swirled through my mind were guaranteed to land me in the electric chair and on an episode of Snapped.

Just as that thought crossed my mind, I let out a guttural scream as I collapsed to my knees. Omar still had access to one of the savings accounts that I had set aside from my dad's life insurance. The account he had access to for bill related purchases had a little over twenty thousand dollars in it. I know it may not seem like much today, but back then it was a small fortune.

While I still had plenty of money in other accounts that he didn't know existed, that was the only money that I ever intended to touch in case of an emergency. It didn't take a genius to conclude that that money was long gone...along with my furniture. A phone call to my credit union confirmed what I already knew to be true. That account had a whooping thirty-eight cents remaining. Whooptie doo, asshole!

How could he do this to me? To our newborn daughter?

For all he knew, that was all the money I had in this world. I missed my dad more now than I ever had before. I could have really used his advice in that moment. He always had a knack for making me feel better. I do not know how long I remained sprawled out on the floor before I heard Lukas's voice.

Snapping out of my trance, I tearfully smiled at him and *our* daughter. Seeing his concerned face assured me that everything would be okay. He and I could make this work. He wasn't Celeste's biological father, but he treated her as his own. He was all she'd gotten to know in her first few weeks of life.

It was he who was up in the middle of the night rocking her back to sleep. It was he who changed her diapers. It was also he who was listed on her birth certificate. He'd done so much for the both of us while Omar had done nothing, but cause me heartache and pain.

As much as I wanted to call the police, Lukas convinced me not to. He told me that he had a little 'street justice' in store for Omar. One look at his face told me he was furious. I knew he had the situation handled and I also knew that my daughter would NEVER meet her biological father. His days were numbered and my frozen heart wouldn't allow me to care.

A week later, I was lounging on the couch breastfeeding Celeste when Lukas walked in. Lukas had replaced everything in my house the same day that I discovered everything missing. It was even better than the old stuff.

Luke was so overprotective and rarely allowed the two of us out of his sight. If he had to go somewhere, he'd have one of his friends watch over us. I was ready to resume my old life. I missed school. I missed my crappy job. I missed Paige. I was tired of being cooped up and catered to like an invalid.

"Hey, how's my two favorite ladies doing?!" Luke inquired as he walked over to the couch and kissed both me and Celeste on our foreheads.

"Hi sweetheart! I'm just feeding this greedy baby of yours! She is going to be big as a house at this rate!" I joked.

"Don't be talking about my baby girl like that. She just has a good appetite like her Papa. Isn't that right Cee Cee?!" He stated unknowingly removing her from my breast.

I blushed briefly as I noted his eyes widen as he caught a quick glimpsed of my erect nipple as our daughter unlatched leaving me momentarily exposed. I hurriedly pulled my shirt down and glanced down into my lap. I could feel his eyes on me, yet I refused to look in his direction.

After he sang and rocked Cee Cee to sleep, he walked down the hall to lay her in her crib. Her nursery was decorated beautifully in pink and white. Once Lukas came back grinning from ear to ear, I walked shyly into the kitchen to warm up his plate of food I had prepared earlier.

I had made fried chicken, homemade macaroni and cheese, cabbage, corn bread and candied yams. Lukas loved my cooking. I even made his favorite lemon-lime Kool-Aid. His eyes lit up as I slowly made my way back into the living room.

"Hungry are we? I told you, you and your baby are GREEDY!" I giggled setting his plate and glass of Kool-Aid down in front of him.

Before I could walk away, he grabbed my hand and gently pulled me onto his lap. My body immediately tensed up at the feel of his erection poking me in my behind.

He playfully tickled me as I squirmed like a child on his lap.

"I told you to stop talking about my baby. She is perfect with her little chunky self." He stated as he continued to tickle me.

After begging for mercy and promising to stop teasing Cee Cee about her insatiable appetite, he finally stopped tickling me. He still wouldn't allow me to get up from his lap.

"Luke, your food is going to get cold. Aren't you hungry?" I asked trying to divert his attention to anything but me.

He became serious. "I am hungry and I am going to eat in a minute. But before I do, I just wanted to tell you how much I love having the two of you here. I didn't realize it until you two came along. I do not ever want a day to go by without me seeing my daughter. You got that G?" He seriously asked as his warm breath made the hair on the back of my neck stand at attention.

I felt his soft lips land on my neck as his right hand landed on my right breast. I was completely caught off guard, yet turned all the way on. My attempt to stifle the loud groan that escaped my lips was in vain. I leaned my head back onto his shoulder as he continued to feast on my neck.

By this time he had lifted my shirt up and was twirling his fingers around my nipple. With each stroke, my tits involuntarily expelled fresh milk. I was self-conscious about it and was telling him to stop so that I could clean myself up. He responded by gently laying me down on the couch.

He sat down on his knees and peered at me lovingly. I could feel his love for me permeate into my soul. It turned me on that much further. As strange as it may sound, Lukas and I had never had sex. We were never able to consummate our marriage.

Because I delivered Celeste so quickly, my body wasn't quite ready for her to come. She was two weeks early and came out as soon as I reached the hospital. She tore me from the inside out. I still had a few weeks before I was scheduled for my six week checkup.

This meant that I had yet to receive the green light to resume sexual activity. The thought of ripping open those stiches during sex terrified me! I needed to get away from my husband and fast!

Shaking my head I replied, "Luke we can't... I'm not ready. The doctor said..."

He popped my right breast into his mouth and I drew a sharp breath in.

"Oh my God Lukas! Mmmmmmmm! Damn!" I belted out.

"Damn your milk taste good as hell. Now I see why Cee Cee stays latched onto those big pretty muthafuckas! So are you gonna finally make love to your man? Hunh?" He stated with his mouth still full of my titty.

If it didn't feel so amazing, I know I would've laughed at the sight in front of me.

"No Lukas, it isn't ti..!!!" I screamed out as he began to massage my clit through my spandex shorts.

I was in pure ecstasy and in between moans I couldn't help, but to wonder why Omar was never able to make me feel this way. He had never been able to get me off. Lukas had just made me cum twice and I still had my shorts on!

After my second orgasm, Lukas once again asked me to make love to him, but again I turned down his advances.

At some point I felt Lukas pulling my shorts and panties down. I told myself I would get freaky with him, but I would not have sex with him. I could please my husband without having sex. Couldn't I?

When he face planted into my juicy center, I thought I'd died and joined my parents in heaven. Omar had certainly never done anything like that before. He thought it was gross. Lukas had me screaming and gyrating my hips all over his face. I'm almost certain I suffocated him a few times as well.

How do women function in the world when feelings, such as the ones he was giving me existed? I was hooked. I just wanted to have my twat eaten all day...every day. After about thirty minutes of him eating me out and asking if I was going to 'give him some', I felt his erection tapping up against my clit.

This alarmed me. Thoughts of how painful having sex with Lukas would be had me trying to push him to the side so that I could sit up. He was having none of that.

"Baby chill out. I'm not gonna hurt you. Come on." He said picking my nude body up and carrying me upstairs to our bedroom. He pulled the covers down in one swift motion and laid me down onto our king sized bed.

"Luke, I haven't been cleared to do this yet. I still have a couple weeks to go. You know I had to get those stitches after having Cee Cee. You might rip me back open with that monster you're working with! I'm not ready. I'm scared." I stated honestly.

"I understand what you're saying completely. I would never hurt you and I'll go slowly. You are ready. *WE* are ready. I feel how wet you are...G, you're ready. I love you and I'm here for the long haul. You are my wife, baby girl I have needs. I have been extremely patient.

Do you realize how difficult it has been being around you, yet not being about to feel you completely? I've never felt this way about a woman. Your young ass is turning me into a sucka! Don't be afraid because you know I got you. Okay?"

I paused for a moment and thought about everything he had said. I truly didn't know what to do. I had loved that man for a long time...longer than I am comfortable admitting to. I have come to realize that he had grown a lot in my absence.

He was in school full-time. He had given up his illegal activities and had opened up a legitimate business. He had done all of those things to become a better man for me. I certainly wanted him in me and Cee Cee's lives forever. She deserved to have a family...a father figure.

Peering up into Lukas's eyes, I slowly nodded my head. "Yes, baby I trust you. I want to be a good wife to you. I want to always please you because I do not want you finding love and affection out there in those streets. Please go slow..."

"Yes!!!" He howled while kissing me all over my face.

"You've made me the happiest man in the world G!!! He exclaimed.

I smiled and proceeded to kiss him back while suckling on his bottom lip.

I felt him take his member and rub it back and forth across my drenched opening. I was afraid to look down. He felt huge!

Once he was satisfied with my wetness, I begin to feel pressure and stretching as he slowly sank into my velvety walls. The pain was worse than my very first time with Omar. I tightly gripped Lukas's back and clawed the hell out of it. He didn't appear to be bothered by me clawing at his back. With each stroke I'd inch away from him until he pinned me down with both his arms and body weight.

"Unh unh. Where do you think you are going baby? Is this my pussy? Hunh? You better not EVER give my shit away again. You got that?!" Luke stated seriously in between strokes.

In between moans, I responded with yes.

Lukas kept his word and went very slow. Every once in a while he'd pick up his speed, but would immediately slow down once he'd note my discomfort. I tried to put my big girl panties on and take it, but I could literally feel him in my stomach. My husband had a horse dick.

"Owww Lukas! You are killing me! Please hurry up baby!" I begged.

"Are you sure you want me to cum?" He asked.

"Yes, baby, cum for me!" I confirmed.

"Okay, I will." He agreed.

Lukas picked up the pace as he proceeded to stroke in and out of me. I was moaning so loudly that it was a miracle that I didn't wake my child up.

Lukas belted a loud, "Fuck!!!" before his body went into convulsions.

My sweaty body exhaustedly went flaccid as I struggled to catch my haggard breath.

Glancing over, I realized that Lukas was staring at me flashing his beautiful pearly whites.

"Luke, why are you being so creepy right now?" I inquired.

"I'm just happy, that's all. I am one lucky bastard and I know it. I do not want my daughter ever being around that nigga. I meant what I said about you being mine now. I'll never let you go...I'd kill you before I allow that to happen.

Oh yeah, you are now pregnant with my son. I paid close attention to your body. I know that you are ovulating right now. I also know that women are extremely fertile right after giving birth. I've just planted my seed and you will keep him. Consider this your way of saying that you're sorry for getting pregnant by someone else." He seriously stated.

I laid there in stunned silence. There was no reason to actually look and see if he'd truly came inside of me. Not only could I feel it dripping back towards my asshole, but I now realized he never pulled out of me. I should've known better. I'm smarter than this!

Rolling onto my side, I ignored Lukas as I brainstormed ways to end this potential pregnancy. There was no way in hell that I was ready for another baby. I was still trying to become acclimated to motherhood. I could NOT be pregnant again! Jesus take the wheel!!!

« Chapter 28 The Normal Baby »

The Past "Gladys"

TRUE TO HIS PROMISE, I was pregnant once again. Here I was this college student who would soon have two young children to care for. Why did this happen? All I wanted to do was finish school so that I could become a teacher. As unprepared as I knew I was for a second child, I knew in my heart that I'd never in good conscience be able to go through with an abortion. I also knew my husband would never allow it.

He was up my ass so much that I knew if I even miscarried; he'd find some way to blame me for it. I'd had brought up the topic of adoption once and he punched a hole in the wall. His temper had become scary after I'd become pregnant. He was very possessive and always appeared to be stressed out. I stood by my man because I knew that he was making some powerful moves.

He had completely changed his life around because I had requested he do so. I wanted for nothing and here I was still complaining. Maybe it was me. Maybe I'm just ungrateful for all that he has done for me. Here I was living the life that most women dreamed of, yet I was whining about being pregnant again. Women would kill to be pregnant by my husband!

I prayed about it. I prayed for God to make me a better wife and mother. I had experienced a mild bout of post partem depression and my current pregnancy seemed to only exacerbate those symptoms. I loved my daughter, but she had been the cause of me sacrificing a lot...even myself at times. I couldn't help but wonder how different my life may have turned out if I hadn't had her. Would I have even married Lukas at all?

Being with Lukas had brought about stability. He accepted Celeste as his own and had legally adopted her. He had showed me very early on that he was more of a man than her own father would ever be. I felt safe from the world when I was with Lukas...however, over time I didn't feel safe from Lukas himself. He has the ability to make me feel like the most beautiful woman to ever grace this Earth and he also had the ability to make me feel lower than the pits of hell.

My pregnancy with my son was a fairly lonely one. Lukas was so wrapped into getting his new businesses off the ground that he often left me and Celeste home alone a lot. He did not allow us to leave much especially with me being pregnant. He was so paranoid that an enemy from his past would retaliate against him through the ones he loved. At the time it made sense, but over time it grew very old.

If it hadn't been for Paige and Shawn's visits, I would've lost my mind. Her son was a beautiful curly haired little boy. He was biracial with honey colored eyes and the cutest set of dimples. She was so heavy into prostituting herself when she conceived him, that she was never able to pinpoint who his biological father was. Paige had finally saved enough money and had opened up her own real estate agency.

I was so happy because I hated her profession. I worried about her constantly. The only downside was that she had become so consumed with her new business that she had dropped out of college. She stated that there wasn't any need to go any further when she had already obtained her career. I wasn't happy with her decision but I would support my friend regardless.

It was through her thriving business that she met the amazing man who would one day become her husband. Scott was also a real estate agent who had come to Paige looking for a job. He was a blond haired, blue eyed stud. They hit it off immediately and fell madly in love. He had even persuaded Paige to regain full custody of Shawn. I was so happy for my friend. I was even happier when she and her budding family were able to swoop in and purchase the house next to ours.

The day that I went into labor is a day that I will never forget. Lukas had finally returned home after a week long hiatus. I still had five weeks remaining until my due date. We were expecting a horrible blizzard and he wanted to ensure that Celeste and I had enough food, water and supplies to make it through. He came just in time, because shortly after his arrival, the power was wiped out. Luckily, candles, flashlights and batteries were among the supplies he'd purchased.

The snow quickly started to fall shortly after he arrived and it did not take long before the snow had literally trapped us inside of my house. I had been having some cramping and had decided to take a warm bubble bath to relax my muscles. I sat in the tub for over a half hour with no relief. I finally decided to get out and try lying down. As I stood up, I felt a gush of fluid dripping out of me and down my legs.

Fear gripped me. We were trapped inside of the house and the phone lines were down so I wouldn't be able to call for assistance.

"Oh God no! Not now, not like this!!!" I cried.

Reaching down, I could feel a hard lump protruding from my vulva. Fine hairs could be felt on the lump. I tried to calm myself down. I was in excruciating pain and I loathed being in the dark. I managed to limp out of the tub and into the doorway. I whispered for Lukas to come into the bathroom so that I wouldn't startle and wake a sleeping Celeste.

Lukas met me in the doorway with a flashlight and asked me what was wrong.

"Luke, my water just broke! What am I supposed to do? I can't have our baby here...with no pain medicine." I squealed in pain.

Lukas lowered the flashlight to my vagina and kneeled down in front of me.

"Damn baby, I can see the head already. There isn't enough time. It's time for you to start pushing. Let me grab some water, towels, blankets and scissors and I'll be right back." He stated calmly.

All I could do is nod my head and cry as I attempted to mentally prepare myself to give birth to my baby on the same floor my father had died on. I'm sure Lukas returned in record breaking time, yet it seemed like an eternity. I had a kid hanging halfway out of my snatch and would be delivering it without the assistance of medical professionals.

Lukas has completely taken over and seemed as if he delivered babies for a living. He had given me a few shots of whiskey and had instructed me when to push and when to breath. He wiped the sweat off my face when I needed it and fed me ice chips.

The entire process took approximately twenty minutes from start to finish. After my final push, I was completely spent. My children didn't believe in waiting before making their entrances into the world. Lukas quickly wrapped our baby up in towels and cut the umbilical cord. Lukas discarded the after birth and then returned to the bathroom to get both me and the baby cleaned up.

Since the baby was quiet and content, he decided to get me together first. He grabbed a washcloth and cleaned in between my thighs. He then assisted me to bed after giving me a pad and some granny panties to wear. After I was squared away, it dawned on the both of us that in our excitement we had failed to notice what the sex of our new baby was. Placing our baby onto the bed and carefully unwrapping it, Lukas aimed the flashlight on it. Even I could see the shocked look displayed on his face in the darkness.

His shock scared the hell out of me. Did I really want to know the reason behind that look?

"Baby, what's wrong? Is it a girl after all?" I tried to lighten the mood knowing that he wanted a boy.

Instead of responding with a verbal response, Lukas simply pointed at our baby.

Although I was beyond sore, I had to investigate what was wrong with my baby. Slowly sitting up, my eyes first counted my baby's toes. I counted ten. My eyes work their way up and I saw his scrotum and penis. No problems there. I then proceeded to count ten fingers and let out a sigh of relief. Lastly I glanced at my son's face and my mouth too fell open.

Our son appeared to be suffering from what is now called a cleft lip and cleft palate. The initial sight of it was shocking at first, but soon I just saw my baby for the beautiful being that he was. After a few moments, his deformity couldn't even alter the love that I now had for him. He was gorgeous and looked just like Lukas. I was in love.

"Bitch are you fucking kidding me?! Is this shit supposed to be funny? That little ugly muthafucka is not my son. Who have you been fucking?!" He barked loudly startling both children.

"You cannot be serious right now Lukas! He is your son! I haven't been with anyone else! How could you say those words to me. To *me*?!" I sobbed.

Lukas swiftly wrapped his arms around my neck and squeezed. "So, you can give that punk ass nigga Omar a normal baby but you give me this retarded ass piece of shit when I've been here for you. That bastard will never have my name and will never be my son. Either you kill his ass or I will kill all three of you." He stated pointing the flashlight at me and then both of my babies.

After releasing my neck, he roughly mushed me in the face.

"If anyone asks, you miscarried. I will go and get some help for you to make sure that you're okay. You cannot go to a hospital because they will ask too many questions. No one will ever know about this shit and I mean it. You have three days to take care of his ass. I don't need details, he just better be gone when I return!" With that, he walked his crazy ass out into the blizzard leaving me alone with two babies.

« Chapter 29 The Great Escape »

The Past "Autumn"

DON HAD OFFICIALLY LOST his damn mind! He had proposed and asked me to marry him. Of course he had technically asked my mother to marry him since he asked, "Celeste, will you please do me the honor of becoming my beautiful wife."

Naturally I told him no. I was honest and told him that I didn't love him and never would.

"Oh Celeste, you have always been so stubborn. I'm ready to tell the world about us now. I'm no longer ashamed of your past. You've change for the better. The only problem is, I know my mother will never accept us as a couple. She will stand in the way of our happiness and for that reason, she must go.

My mother has always been good to me and I do not wish to bring her any pain or suffering. However, I've put my life on hold for too long just to appease others. It is time for me to start living and I cannot do that if I am disinherited or behind bars for statutory rape.

Did this fool just say statutory? The sex was always pretty damn forcible in my opinion. Ever since he revealed his plan to kill Mrs. Douglas, I had been working overtime to find an alternative living arrangement. My dad had called me a couple of weeks ago to tell me that his beloved wife had died from uterine cancer.

Apparently they had discovered a mass during her pregnancy with Justice, but she refused to receive any treatments until after she had delivered my little sister. Unfortunately, her pregnancy and elevated hormone levels had accelerated and metastasized her cancer. By the time she was ready for treatment, it was already too late. Chemo and radiation could've bought her a little more time but she had opted against it.

What time she had, she refused to be doped up and sick. She had chosen quality over quantity. Although I couldn't stand the woman for her treatment of both my sister and I, I couldn't help but to admire her strength and bravery. It did make me understand why she didn't want Wintress and I around. Had my dad been honest from the beginning, I would've understood.

I felt slightly guilty for taking advantage of my father during what I'm sure was one of the most difficult times of his life, but I had to get away from Don! I had made him promise not to repeat anything that I was about to tell him. I told him everything just as I had told MaDonna. By the end of my confession, I could hear him crying on the other end of the receiver.

He apologized over and over again. He promised to step up to the plate and finally offer Wintress and I the help we so desperately needed. Just hearing this put my heart at ease. I was able to sleep a little better knowing that the end was approaching.

It was bittersweet. I was going to hate leaving the boys behind. I knew that they were safe here, but I had grown to love them as my true siblings. I knew me and my sister were already pushing our luck by asking my dad for a place to stay. I didn't have it in me to ask if the boys could come too. Plus they probably would never want to leave Mrs. Douglas anyway. They worshipped and adored her so much.

I couldn't help but to smile as I thought about how this time next week, we would be far away from this hell hole. I promised my dad that we wouldn't be a burden and that we'd leave as soon as I turned eighteen. I even sold him on the idea of having free babysitters for Justice.

∞

Three days after my conversation with my dad, there was a loud knock on the front door. Before I could make it to the door, Mrs. Douglas and Don opened the door and were met by my case worker, Kelly and a police officer.

I could hear Kelly ask, "May we come in?"

I never heard a response back, but I watched as the two of them walked in.

The four of them walked into the family room and sat down on the couch.

"I'm sure you are curious as to why we are here so I will not keep you in suspense. I received a call from Autumn's biological father, Micah-Shawn Taylor. He prefers to be called Shawn. He told me that Autumn told him that she is being raped by you, Mr, Douglas. She also reports that you have even gotten her pregnant and forced her to have an underground abortion. Lastly she reported that Wintress is your biological daughter Mr. Douglas. Is there any truth to any of these allegations?"

"That is absolutely absurd! Don would do no such thing! I cannot believe you came all the way here to ask us such ridiculous questions!" Mrs. Douglas shrieked clutching her chest.

"Again, *Mr. Douglas*, is there any truth to these allegations?" Kelly asked again making it clear that she only wanted an answer from Don.

"Kelly, those allegations are completely false. I'd never do those things to Autumn or to any child. I've been nothing but nice to Autumn since she's arrived. I apologize that she's wasted your time coming down here."

"Be that as it may, due to the severity of these allegations, we will have to remove all four children from the home immediately pending an investigation. We will interview all of the children and I'm sure a DNA test will be ordered in order to discredit the paternity allegation.

You seem like good people and I'm sure that there is nothing to this but I cannot ignore the allegations. Shawn is seeking full custody of both Autumn and Wintress. He is threatening to go to the authorities and the news if these children are left in your care. The girls will most likely be placed with him once the investigation is finished. The boys will be placed back with you if everything checks out. Can you gather the children for me?" Kelly stated.

"You simply can't be serious! Those children are not going anywhere with you! Those are our kids. We've done nothing wrong. Now please leave our home!" Mrs. Douglas shrieked.

"Mrs. Douglas, I completely understand your frustrations, however it is beyond our control. If our investigation comes back clean, the children will be returned. Now please, I do not want this to get ugly. Get the children now!" The officer finally chimed in.

"As my mother as already explained to the both of you, these children aren't going anywhere!" Don boomed drawing a gun from between the couch cushion.

The officer followed suit, however, the officer clumsily fumbled with his nine, nearly dropping it. In his attempt to catch his gun, he accidentally discharged a single shot. That shot somehow found its way through little Landon's heart instantly killing him.

The house was completely silent and still for a brief moment before all hell broke loose. Mrs. Douglas was the first one to react.

"Oh my God! No, not my baby! You've killed my baby! You son-of-a-bitch, you've killed my baby!!!" She chanted over and over again as she made her way over to his motionless body.

I slapped my hands over my mouth as I watched as Don angrily unloaded his gun into the officer, Kelly and then his own momma. He had killed them all execution style. I noticed both Wintress and Chris standing stunned in a nearby corner. Silent tears streamed down their innocent faces. I knew that Don was preoccupied with the four corpses lying on the ground so it was now or never for the three of us to make our great escape.

Creeping over to Chris and Wintress, I led them both over to a side door near the dining room. I quietly unlocked the door and allowed the children to slip out of the door first. Once they made it out, I quickly followed suit. I whispered for them both to run as hard and as fast as they could because our lives depended on it.

« Chapter 30 Victim Of Circumstances »

The Past "Eli"

LATELY, I HAD BEEN KICKING it with Pinky real tough. I knew she could never be my top bitch again because she had kids and shit now. I knew she was battling her inner demons right now. Even though Trey was a piece of shit, she genuinely loved that nigga for some reason. I knew it wasn't easy for her to give him up to me.

It's safe to say Gia's pregnancy had scared the hell out of me. I wasn't fucking around like I typically did and I made sure to always stay strapped up. That was a close ass call. I never wanted to go through anything like that ever again. I had been dodging Gia like the plague. She'd never taste this dick ever again. The pussy was good, but not good enough to be ordered to pay child support for. No fucking way!

I had finally started talking to my little sister again. I made sure to keep a super close eye on both her and my brother. Apparently I had become so engrossed in my own life and hustling that I had forgotten to be there for them physically. I had met all of their financial needs and wants but what they needed the most was me.

I had talked my sister into joining the swim team in order to occupy most of her free time. She was beautiful, but naïve and I didn't want any of these other bum ass niggas having the opportunity to sink their claws into her. I scheduled family nights and ensured that she reported her whereabouts at all times. The leash that I had my siblings on was less than an inch long. Malia had to earn my trust back.

School was school. I wasn't the best student but I certainly wasn't the worst. I had never been crazy about school but I was intelligent enough to know that a college education was necessary. I had to have a backup plan.

I had run into Cee Cee at the mall a few days ago and as always, I stared at her with lust in my eyes. I still hadn't figured out the right approach to win her back. She still gave me the stink eye whenever we crossed paths. I hated rejection and really hated her putting her hands on me the last time I tried to apologize to her.

I knew I deserved it, but the shit hurt and I had nearly snapped and hit her back. Celeste has been abused all her life and that is the very last thing she needed...another abuser.

I had been hearing some disturbing rumors about Cee Cee lately and I prayed that they were truly just rumors. I had heard that she was popping pills and was pretty strung out on them. People around the way had told me that she'd attempted to cop from them on several different occasions.

This shit spooked me. I know that I sniffed my fair share of coke, but those pills seemed to be taking people out left and right. The mortality rate seemed higher with pills than with coke. I had to talk to her and see for myself. I hated rumors.

"Hey Cee Cee, long time, no see beautiful. How have you been baby?" I asked leaning down to hug her.

I was surprised when she actually wrapped her arms around me in return.

"I've been better. How are you Eli?" She asked sadly.

"Fuck how I'm doing...what's going on baby?" I asked genuinely concerned.

"Oh gosh, it's a long story. I'll get through it."

"Cee Cee, I have nothing but time for you. You are not leaving without telling me what's going on with you." I stated.

I couldn't help noticing that she had grown even more beautiful in my absence. She was perfection, but the light in her eyes seemed dull today.

"Just everything Eli. I'm tired of living. I hate my life. Long story short, my dad got me hooked on pills. Not directly but as a result of him pushing me down those stairs. I was in so much pain that sometimes I had to double and triple up for relief. Before I realized what was happening, I woke up one day and couldn't go without them without getting sick. I've tried shaking this shit, but I just can't. I almost lost my fucking job behind this shit. Pills are so hard to come by.

Eli can you help me? I need to find something else besides these pills. I need something more accessible. I will not do the shit forever, I just need something that can tide me over before I lose my job and flunk out of school. My parents cannot find out or they will kill me. I cannot focus on anything but how I will obtain pills. Help me Eli, please!" She begged.

"Damn Cee Cee, we can get you into a rehab or something. I do not want to create more problems for you baby. Please don't ask me to do this! I won't!" I bellowed.

"Eli, if you do not help me, I will kill myself. I am dead serious too! I promise I will do it!" She hissed.

Letting out a frustrated sigh, I ran my hands over my face. I couldn't believe that she was asking this of me.

Looking at her I stated, "Here's the deal. I will help you out but only for a month. I only fuck with coke. You do not cop from anyone but me because you do not know what that shit is laced with out there. After a month, you will get help. Follow me to my house so that I can show you the proper way to use it. Damn Cee Cee...fuck!" I exclaimed hating being put into this position. I prayed for God to bring me back my girl, but this isn't what I had in mind.

∞

Tonight was the night. I was out for redemption. It had taken years, but I was now ready to make a move. My hatred for that nigga had peaked to an all-time high. His face now invaded my dreams and I found it impossible to rest knowing that he was still roaming around inhaling the same air that I was permitted to.

Years ago this asshole had forever changed the course of my life. I wasn't always this way. Circumstances had brought me to this place. Hell, I was the victim in all this. A victim of my circumstances. I didn't like hustling the way that I did but I didn't see any other way. Life gave me lemons and I had made some sweet ass lemonade.

Lately it seemed as if everything was turning into shit. My sister's fast ass had gotten caught fucking an older nigga, my little brother was soft as hell and would most likely skip out of a closet in the near future, my granny was getting old and Celeste...where would I even start with her.

Finally, I had a clear shot of him. Of course, he had his main bitch with him. She disgusted me as much as he did. They were walking with their backs towards me. I had my gun cocked and was more than ready to fill his ass with lead. I had envisioned and fantasized about this very moment hundreds of times before.

Not wanting to kill him without him knowing who did it and why, I loudly cleared my throat to announce my presence.

"Hey nigga, turn your old ass around slowly! Put your muthafucking hands up in the air too! Bitch you too!" I barked tingling with excitement.

"Muthafucka you must not know who I..." He stopped talking once he saw my face.

"Do you recognize me?" I asked already knowing the answer.

"Yeah you are that little muthafucka that I kicked out of my daughter's hospital room. Man what the fuck are you doing here and what the fuck do you want?!" He replied annoyed by my presence.

His bitch's eyes were glued to me. Her mouth was open wide in stunned silence.

"Yes and no. I am the guy that you saw in Cee Cee's hospital room, however, we go back so much further than that nigga. Look at me closely. I know it will come to you if you just study my features closely. I'll even throw you a hint; I look just like my pops. Now I know you wouldn't forget the face of anyone that you've killed right? If you are gonna kill a nigga at least have enough respect to remember their face." I spat.

The look of annoyance slowly left his face as a look of horror took over.

"Yes, I see you aren't as stupid as you look muthafucka. Eli, also known as Big E was my pops. You were jealous and threatened by my pop's status and money. You wanted to be him. You wanted his bitch, his paper, his streets and his power. You couldn't play fair and share the streets like most niggas...you had to have it all. Payback is a bitch, did you not think that this day would eventually come? I'm named after my pops, there's no way that I wouldn't avenge his death.

You set my pops up and like the little bitch you are, you tried to step into his shoes. You will never be half the man my pops was. You know, sometimes it takes everything in me not to blow my little brother's brains out because the older he gets, the more he looks like you. Let's not forget how you use to beat me and fuck me in the ass when I was younger.

My hatred for you runs so deep. I wish that I could kill and revive you a thousand times and even then that wouldn't be enough. You beat and tortured my girl her entire life. You even got her strung out of pills and shit now. You kidnapped my mother, brainwashed her, took her away from us and turned her into one of your hoes. Any last words muthafucka?"

"Man little nigga fuck you! You're a bitch just like Big E's weak ass was. I'm not about to beg and plead for my life. Fuck all this reminiscing shit and do what you came here to do, otherwise, get the fuck on and let us be on our way!" He stated grabbing his woman.

"My nigga, fuck you too!!!" Is all I remembered shouting before releasing a series of shots in his direction.

Once emptying my clip, I walked over to the body lying on the ground. As my eyes focused on the body, I realized that the son of a bitch had used his bitch as a shield. I then heard tires screeching away from the scene. I could only assume that it was Lukas's bitch ass making his escape.

Looking at the beautiful woman lying on the ground, I couldn't help but to sit down next to her and place her head onto my lap. Tears were flowing freely as I stroked her lifeless cheek.

"I am so sorry Ma. I never meant to hurt you. I know you were far from perfect, but I would have never hurt you intentionally. Please forgive me." I cried.

I gave her a peck on her forehead and gently laid her head back down onto the pavement. Hearing sirens blaring in the distance, I knew that I'd have to finish grieving elsewhere. Racing to my car, I nearly had a heart attack as a half dozen cop cars surrounded my vehicle.

TO BE CONTINUED...

My Wife's Daughters

Is Coming soon!!!

INEVITABLE DECEPTIONS 2

CPSIA information can be obtained
at www.ICGtesting.com
Printed in the USA
LVHW011834080119
603173LV00021B/453/P